Savin' Up for Saturday Night
THE HONKY-TONK MUSICAL

Book by Jeff Goode

Songs by Richard Levinson

A SAMUEL FRENCH ACTING EDITION

SAMUEL FRENCH

FOUNDED 1830

SAMUELFRENCH.COM

RENTAL MATERIALS

An orchestration consisting of **Piano/Conductor Score, Vocal Scores, and a Demo CD** will be loaned two months prior to the production ONLY on the receipt of the Licensing Fee quoted for all performances, the rental fee and a refundable deposit.

Please contact Samuel French for perusal of the music materials as well as a performance license application.

IMPORTANT BILLING AND CREDIT REQUIREMENTS

All producers of *SAVIN' UP FOR SATURDAY NIGHT must* give credit to the Authors of the Play in all programs distributed in connection with performances of the Play, and in all instances in which the title of the Play appears for the purposes of advertising, publicizing or otherwise exploiting the Play and/or a production. The names of the Authors *must* appear on a separate line on which no other name appears, immediately following the title and *must* appear in size of type not less than fifty percent of the size of the title type.

DR. BARTENDER
Music and Lyrics by Richard Levinson © 1981 Tinnitus Music

SAVIN' UP FOR SATURDAY NIGHT
Music and Lyrics by Richard Levinson © 2000 Black Toast Music

LET ME SHOW YOU WHAT HE'S MISSING TONIGHT
Music and Lyrics by Richard Levinson, Randall Cate and DeWayne Blackwell
© 1980 Universal Music Group

DANCE FLOOR DEMONS
Music and Lyrics by Richard Levinson © 2002 Tinnitus Music

NOW I'M SWINGIN'
Music by Richard Levinson and Joel Wachbrit.
Lyrics by Richard Levinson © 2006 Tinnitus Music/Black Toast Music/ Calamari Music

TRYING TO GET OVER ME
Music and Lyrics by Richard Levinson © 2002 Tinnitus Music

SHE WANTED TO BE A SINGER
Music by Thomas Rucker Campbell Lyrics by Richard Levinson
© 1981 Tinnitus Music/WTRC Music

TOO EARLY FOR THE BLUES
Music and Lyrics by Richard Levinson © 2010 Tinnitus Music

LET'S DO SOMETHING CHEAP AND SUPERFICIAL
Music and Lyrics by Richard Levinson © 1979 Music Publishing Company of America

SMALL TOWN
Music and Lyrics by Richard Levinson © 1981 Tinnitus Music

COME ON, LUCINDA
Music and Lyrics by Richard Levinson © 2003 Tinnitus Music

IF YOU DON'T TELL HER
Music and Lyrics by Richard Levinson © 2004 Tinnitus Music

WHEN WE DANCE
Music by Thomas Rucker Campbell Lyrics by Richard Levinson
© 1981 Tinnitus Music/WTRC Music

SAVIN' UP FOR SATURDAY NIGHT opened at the Sacred Fools Theater in Los Angeles, California on September 18, 2009. The performance was directed by Jeremy Aldridge, with sets by David Knutson, costumes by Jaimie Froemming, lighting by Yancy Dunham, sound by Chris Millar, choroegraphy by Allison Bibicoff, props by Lisa Ann Nicolai, and fight choreography by Laura Napoli. The Production Stage Manager was Suze Campagna. The cast was as follows:

DOC . . . . Bryan Krasner

LUCINDA . . . . Natascha Corrigan

ELDRIDGE. . . . . Brendan Hunt

PATSY . . . . Courtney DeCosky

RODDY . . . . Dave Fraser

SISSY . . . . Rachel Howe

DANCERS . . . . Ceasar F. Barajas, Mike Kluck, Gregg Moon,
Don Baker, Rhonda Diamond, Gina Tucci, & Natasha Norman

THE BAND

John Groover McDuffie . . . . Musical Director / Guitar / Pedal Steel

Peter Freiberger . . . . Bass / Pedal Steel

Dave Fraser . . . . Piano

John Palmer . . . . Drums

Al Bonhomme . . . . Guitar Alternate

PRODUCTION STAFF

Producers . . . . J.J. Mayes, Brian Wallis, & Terry Tocantins

Associate Producers . . . . Richard Levinson & Jason Charnick

Assistant Director . . . . Ruth Silveira

Assistant Choreographers . . . . Rhonda Diamond & Don Baker

Vocal Coach . . . . Rachel Howe

Assistant Stage Manager . . . . Christy Bunner

Light Board Op . . . . Suze Campagna

Sound Board Op . . . . Ari Radousky

Graphic Design / Photography . . . . Jason Charnick

Understudies . . . . Paul Byrne, Mandy Kaplan, Michael Canaan,
Rachel Howe, & Erika Whalen

CHARACTERS

ELDRIDGE - The owner of the Bar & Fill and front man for the bar band; a country star wannabe who never did.

LUCINDA - Eldridge's ex-wife, ex-singing partner, and former high school sweetheart; now a single mother and regular barfly, but still the best dancer in town.

DOC - The bartender and peacekeeper at the Ready Bar & Fill; Eldridge's best friend since childhood and the best man at his wedding. Doc walks with a limp from a high school traffic accident, when Eldridge was driving.

PATSY - The hapless waitress at the Bar & Fill and Eldridge's new partner-in-song.

RODDY - The Bar & Fill's long-suffering musician, mechanic, and fry cook.

OPTIONAL CHORUS OF BAR PATRONS AND DANCERS - small-town locals in for a beer and a line dance, and out-of-town travelers who broke down on the highway.

SETTING

The Ready Bar & Fill, a one-stop honky-tonk and auto body shop in the tiny town of Ready, U.S.A.

AUTHORS' NOTES

Savin' Up for Saturday Night was originally conceived and written to be performed in a Chicago bar and cabaret space with a single piano for accompaniment and a cast of four actors singing and dancing with the audience in an intimate setting.

When the play premiered in Los Angeles, it was at a larger 99-seat black box theatre, which had been remodeled to accommodate the show. Stadium seating was removed and replaced with bar tables, converting the theatre itself into a working bar with a live house band in an environmental staging. A chorus of dancers was added to the ensemble to portray bar patrons, and perform an expanded slate of dance numbers, some of which were partially-improvised to allow for audience participation.

The critically-acclaimed production then moved to an even larger, conventional proscenium theatre, which allowed for an even bigger dance ensemble, but less audience interaction. The play was re-blocked and choreographed for the proscenium stage, and framing songs and scenework were added to recognize the separation of the "fourth wall."

Throughout the development of the play, the authors have tried to make sure that even as the show was expanded and adapted to larger and more elaborate venues that it also maintains the flexibility to play in smaller, intimate spaces as well.

Thus, the musical you hold in your hands can be performed with a large company of dancers, or just the core cast of four actors and Roddy; accompanied by a full country band, or a single musician on piano, guitar or accordion; as an immersive theatre experience where the audience find themselves rubbing elbows with the characters in a small town bar, or in a proscenium setting where the audience can sit back and enjoy the spectacle of the town of Ready coming to life up on the stage.

Whether the venue is large or small, conventional theatre or a found space, *Savin' Up for Saturday Night* is designed to provide an evening of entertainment that can fill any stage. Directors and producers are encouraged to consider the options that will best suit your theatre, your company and your talent pool.

SONGWRITER'S NOTES

The score to *Savin' Up For Saturday Night* consists entirely of country and honky-tonk songs. The show was originally written for five actors, one of whom (Roddy) also accompanies all of the songs on piano. The parts/lead sheets and CD are provided for a cast of this size. However, for the World Premiere, a four-piece country band was used. The following notes will be helpful in producing the show with the original accompaniment or with a band of any type or size.

CD and Parts

The CD includes piano / vocal demos of all of the songs in the show, in show order, and the printed parts correspond to these piano demos as to key and arrangement. The recordings and printed parts should be used together to prepare for performance.

It is not necessary that any or all of the actors read music... some of the best country musicians and singers don't. In the case of "by-ear" performers, the CD and lyrics within the script will be plenty to learn the songs and develop them. These are road maps – individual interpretations of the songs are encouraged.

The CD also contains recordings of several of the songs as performed at live stagings, and several studio recordings by others as well. These do not necessarily conform in arrangement or key with the printed parts, but are included to offer examples of how some bands and singers have done the songs.

Except where noted otherwise in the script, all of the songs must be performed, and all of the lyrics must be sung. However, intro and outro lengths, instrumental sections, keys, and tempos may always be changed at the discretion of the Director, Choreographer and Music Director. (Ex. At the World Premiere, an eight-member dance ensemble was onstage for much of the show as customers at the Bar'n'Fill. The last song, "We Gotta Lotta Rockin," was extended instrumentally for lengthened solos which were played behind a raucous final dance that turned into an even more raucous bar fight!)

Any type of country music band can play the music to this show: a Zydeco group with accordion, a bluegrass group, a traditional country band with pedal steel, or any combination. Additional master rhythm charts will be provided upon request.

Note: It is possible that Roddy could be played by a guitar player rather than a piano player, especially within the context of a band.

Types of Song Performances.

There are three types of song performances in Savin' Up...

First, the songs performed by Eldridge or Patsy as part of the "show" at the Bar'n'Fill, which are accompanied by Roddy (or Roddy with the band).

Second, several songs performed by Eldridge and Lucinda using Roddy or a full band, but not as part of Eldridge's show – Lucinda's "Let Me Show You" and "Leave the Dancin' to Me." and Edridge's "Trying to Get Over Me and "Come On, Lucinda." (In the World Premiere, this turned into a full cast/dance production number as well.)

Third, all of the songs sung by Doc, whether solo or duet, are "musical theater'" numbers in which only the singer and the person he is singing to or with are aware of the song... no one else in the cast is in the scene, nor can "hear' them.

To make this distinction, at the World Premiere, the songs in the first two categories were accompanied by the entire band. The "Doc" songs were accompanied only by Roddy, who had previously been "noodling" at the piano to leave the impression that he also was in his own world. Although the actor playing Roddy is in fact playing the music for Doc's songs, Roddy the character is not part of the scene and is not aware of the song being sung.

If Roddy is the solo accompanist, this same effect can be achieved with lighting changes, or any other device a Director may imagine.

Note: The optional song "Too Early For the Blues" is a sort of hybrid as Lucinda is singing it to herself – the instrumental section in this song is envisioned as her own fantasy dance and could well include the whole band, if there is one. They would not be aware of her singing the song and are not part of the scene other than to provide the music accompaniment occurring in her mind.

Background Harmonies

Two duets and the one "trio" section of "I Used to Love the Rain," all in the second act, have background harmony parts provided. The other songs are to be sung solo except:

Roddy, or a band, if used in the show, may add at the Musical Director's discretion standard country harmonies to the choruses of the following songs, all of which are part of Eldridge's "show" or Lucinda taking over the band, all in the first act:

Savin' Up for Saturday Night (the full band recording on the CD includes harmony)
Let Me Show You What He's Missing Tonight
Dance Floor Demons
Now I'm Swingin'

Roddy "Noodling"

There are several spots in the script where Roddy "noodles" at the piano as an underscore to dialogue, usually just before accompanying a song of Doc's or his own. These are improvised, and any appropriate section of music from the show may be used, played in a meandering style softly behind the dialogue. It is advised that the noodling occur in the same key as the song it precedes. The melodies from "Here," "Whatever's Left of Me," or "Let's Do Something Cheap and Superficial," played gently and somewhat haphazardly, have worked well in prior productions.

The Main Thing

Have fun! These are country honky-tonk songs, not grand opera. They are the raw material to be shaped by the cast's personalities and understanding of the style into something alive and exciting! There is no penalty for a band and cast finding their own groove and pushing the songs where they want to take them... the songs can come alive in a number of different ways when singers and musicians contribute their own talents, and the audience will be well rewarded!

MUSICAL NUMBERS

ACT ONE

"Dr. Bartender" ....DOC
"Savin' Up For Saturday Night" ....ELDRIDGE
"Let Me Show Your What He's Missing Tonight" ....LUCINDA
"Dance Floor Demons" ....ELDRIDGE
"Now I'm Swingin'" ....PATSY
"Trying to Get Over Me" ....ELDRIDGE
"She Wanted to be a Singer" ....PATSY
"Too Early For The Blues" (Optional)....................LUCINDA
"Let's Do Something Cheap and Superficial" .... DOC & LUCINDA

ACT TWO

"Small Town" .... DOC & LUCINDA
"Come On, Lucinda" ....ELDRIDGE
"If You Don't Tell Her" ....DOC
"When We Dance" ....PATSY
"I Used to Love the Rain" .... PATSY, DOC, & LUCINDA
"Whatever's Left of Me" .... RODDY
"Leave the Dancin' to Me" ....LUCINDA
"Tourists" .... DOC & LUCINDA
"We Gotta Lotta Rockin' To Do" ....ELDRIDGE
"Here" (Optional) ....PATSY
"Savin' Up For Saturday Night" ....ELDRIDGE AND CAST

The authors would like to thank

Cheryl Snodgrass
&
Brian BonDurant
(The Spot Chicago - www.spotchicago.com)

Diana Martin
Lonny Chapman Group Repertory Theatre

Jaime Andrews, Scott Leggett, & J.J. Mayes
(Sacred Fools Theater Company
Artistic Committee 2008-2009)

ACT I

*(It's almost show time at The Honky Tonk Bar and Fill,
a one-stop gas station and dance hall in the tiny town of
Ready, U.S.A.)*

*(**RODDY** and the band are warming up on stage, as
DOC the bartender limps over to the dressing room and
pounds on the door.)*

DOC. Showtime, Eldridge!

ELDRIDGE. *(offstage)* Five minutes!

DOC. It was five minutes, five minutes ago.

ELDRIDGE. *(offstage)* Ten minutes!

DOC. Ten minutes ain't gonna get you over your hangover.
You want some coffee?

ELDRIDGE. *(offstage)* Only if it's Irish.

*(**DOC** flags down **PATSY** the waitress.)*

DOC. Patsy, you wanna see about gettin' him a little hair o'
the dog? *(sotto voce)* Hold the dog.

PATSY. I'm on it.

*(**PATSY** grabs a coffee pot and grinder, fixes her cleavage,
and ducks into the back room, as **DOC** limps over to the
stage and addresses the waiting crowd.)*

DOC. Sorry for the delay, folks. We're experiencing some
technical difficulties.

(sound of a coffee grinder)

And while our "technician" is fetchin' our "difficulty"
some coffee, let me just welcome you all out to The
Honky Tonk Bar & Fill, where we're famous for two
things: And one of 'em is underpriced gasoline. The
pumps outside are old, and the dials don't go up past

$1.99. So there's a two-drink minimum with every fill and that seems to work out about right. We don't encourage drinkin' and drivin'. But we do encourage drinking. And driving. So ask your waitress if you got any fluids need topped. You tip 'er right, you might get a free oil change. Tip 'er wrong, you'll get your drinks watered down, just like the gas. And I oughta know, cuz I'm your bartender. My friends call me "Doc", and you look a friendly bunch. You don't wanna know what they call me that's not my friends. But let's just say they shouldn't oughta make fun of the handicapped. *(turns to the band)* Roddy?

RODDY. I didn't say nothin'.

DOC. Did you want to say something?

RODDY. No...

DOC. About the fire exits?

RODDY. Oh, yeah.

> (**RODDY** *steps to the front of the stage in greasy coveralls and a chef's apron. He's a little nervous to be in front of such a large crowd, so he forgets what he wanted to say.*)

DOC. Roddy?

RODDY. *(startled)* Yeah, if you folks could leave off your cell phones, I appreciate it. It aggravates my aneurism somethin' awful. And I can't play when I'm havin' a seizure. *(beat)* Is what we come to find out.

DOC. And in case of fire...?

RODDY. Oh, right. And if it's in case o' fire, I just wanna say..."My bad." I probably left my welding torch too close to the fry vats again. Or a lug wrench in the microwave like I did that one time.

DOC. Ahem...

RODDY. Two times.

DOC. And the fire exits are...?

RODDY. Oh, uh...

> (**RODDY** *figures out where the fire exits are.*)

RODDY. They're over there. And that's the bathroom. But you can't get out through that window, if you're wearin' a tool belt. And you don't wanna go through the kitchen, cuz that's probably where the fire's gonna be.

DOC. *(to audience)* But if you think you smell smoke, not to worry, it's prob'ly just the dance floor, and you burnin' it up. So as soon as they're good to go backstage–Patsy!

PATSY. *(offstage)* I'm brewin' as fast as I can!

DOC. *(to audience)* All right, well, sit back and grab yourself a beerfreshment, this'll just take a minute. Or ten. Roddy?

RODDY. Yeah, Doc?

DOC. You better vamp.

RODDY. What'd you call me?

DOC. Roddy!

*(**RODDY** noodles.)*

*(MUSIC IN: **DR. BARTENDER**)*

*(**DOC** ambles over to the bar, adjusts the lighting, and pours another round of drinks.)*

DOC.

THE BAR IS OPEN, IT'S THE SAME OLD CROWD
THE NIGHT IS YOUNG, SO THEY'RE LAUGHING LOUD
NOW I'M THE GUY WHO POURS THE ROUNDS,
DON'T MAKE MUCH, I DO ALRIGHT
BUT I'D BE A RICH MAN IF I GOT PAID
FOR THE SERVICE I PERFORM
WHEN THE SMILES ALL FADE
THEY GIVE DEGREES AT UNIVERSITIES
FOR WHAT I DO EVERY NIGHT

WHEN THEY SAY
DR. BARTENDER, LISTEN TO ME
I NEED SOME CHEAP PSYCHOLOGY
SO PUT A GLASS IN FRONT OF ME
AND LET'S TALK ABOUT MY LIFE

DOC. *(cont.)*

AND THEY SAY DR. BARTENDER, HIT ME AGAIN
WHEN THEY'VE GOT WOUNDS ONLY I CAN MEND
THEY JUST LOOK FOR THE FLASHING NEON LIGHT
THAT SAYS THE BAR IS OPEN
AND THE DOCTOR IS IN TONIGHT

I'M THE ONE THEY COME RUNNING FOR
WHEN THE WORLD DON'T MAKE NO SENSE NO MORE
AND I'M THE ONE WHO THROWS 'EM OUT THE DOOR
WHEN THEY'RE LOOKING FOR A FIGHT
BUT MOSTLY I'M AN ONLY FRIEND
WITH A BEER TO POUR AND AN EAR TO LEND
SO IF YOU GOT A COUPLE BUCKS TO SPEND,
I'M ON CALL TONIGHT

AND THEY SAY
DR. BARTENDER, LISTEN TO ME
I NEED SOME CHEAP PSYCHOLOGY
SO PUT A GLASS IN FRONT OF ME
AND LET'S TALK ABOUT MY LIFE
AND THEY SAY DR. BARTENDER, HIT ME AGAIN
WHEN THEY'VE GOT WOUNDS ONLY I CAN MEND
THEY JUST LOOK FOR THE FLASHING NEON LIGHT
THAT SAYS THE BAR IS OPEN...
THE BAR IS OPEN
AND THE DOCTOR IS IN TONIGHT

*(**LUCINDA** bursts through the front door, dressed for a one woman Girls-Night-Out.)*

LUCINDA. Hey, everybody, there's a storm comin' in.

DOC. You don't gotta brag, Lucinda. We heard you comin' up the street.

LUCINDA. I'm talking about the weather. *(to audience)* Make sure your windows is rolled up, folks, or you're in for damp trousers tonight. *(to an audience member)* That goes double for you, handsome.

*(**LUCINDA** goes to the bar.)*

Evenin', Doc.

DOC. Back for more, Lucinda?

LUCINDA. You know I never can get enough.

DOC. And you don't know when you had too much. I'd ask you to behave yourself, but I see you're not dressed for it.

LUCINDA. What? This old thing?

DOC. That old thing still got the tags on.

(**DOC** *grabs a pair of scissors and helps her off with the price tags.*)

LUCINDA. Nice to see you, too, Doc.

DOC. Never said it wasn't nice.

LUCINDA. Now you're just tryin' to butter me up.

DOC. Whatever gets you buttery, Lucinda.

LUCINDA. You play your cards right, you could have me in the sack by closing time.

DOC. You keep saying that, but I keep goin' home to an empty sack. Margarita?

LUCINDA. You read my mind.

DOC. I read your bar tab. It starts off a margarita, and works on up to body shots over a barstool by closing time.

LUCINDA. Can I help it I'm agile?

DOC. Where's your boy El-three? Not back from his step-grandma's?

LUCINDA. Yeah, but I'm not about to bring him down to the honky tonk for Girls' Night Out. There's certain things a boy should not have to see his momma do to a total stranger. Over a barstool.

DOC. So the gals at the office decided to cut loose tonight?

LUCINDA. Unanimously.

DOC. Cuz, as I recall, you're the only gal at your office, Lucinda.

LUCINDA. That's no reason I should be deprived of my God-given legal right to just wanna have fun!

DOC. So what'd you hire a sitter?

LUCINDA. Nah, that's what relatives are for. El-three's over at his Uncle Tommy's.

DOC. His gay Uncle Tommy? Eldridge is gonna love that.

LUCINDA. If he don't want our boy growin' up with an appreciation for the arts, he's gotta spot me some child support, now and again. I'm not about to sit home on a Saturday night cuz Eldridge don't like my half-brother's taste in musicals. *(to the band)* Hi, Roddy.

RODDY. Ma'am.

LUCINDA. When you gonna come fix my clutch?

RODDY. You gotta bring it on down to the shop. Eldridge says I don't make house calls no more.

LUCINDA. What if I ask you real nice?

RODDY. I can come by tomorrow.

(Meanwhile, DOC has returned to the stage to address the audience.)

DOC. Ladies and Gentlemen, thanks for all your patience. We've got a real special treat for you tonight...And it's the same special treat we have every night here at the Bar & Fill, because his daddy, Eldridge Senior, built the place, back when it was just a car wash. *(shouting backstage)* You about ready?

ELDRIDGE. *(offstage)* Born there, Doc!

DOC. So without any further to do: Here he is! The man you've all been waiting for. Literally waiting. For 'bout ten minutes now.

ELDRIDGE. *(offstage)* I can hear you right through this curtain—!

DOC. *(ignoring him)* Eldridge Juuuuunior!

(MUSIC IN: SAVIN' UP FOR SATURDAY NIGHT)

(ELDRIDGE bursts onto the stage in a glitzy rock star outfit that would have embarrassed Elvis himself. He sings and dances around the stage and out into the audience.)

ELDRIDGE.

    EVERYBODY KNOWS YOU'VE GOT TO SAVE YOUR DOUGH
    'CAUSE YOU'RE GONNA NEED IT SOMEDAY
    SO I WORK HARD ALL WEEK
    AND I STASH MY CASH AWAY
    I'VE GOT A SIMPLE STRATEGY
    I KEEP ONE GOAL IN SIGHT
    I SAVE MY MONEY CAREFULLY
    SO IT WILL BE THERE FOR ME
    WHEN SOMEDAY COMES ALONG THIS SATURDAY NIGHT

    I'M SAVING UP FOR SATURDAY NIGHT
    THAT'S THE BEST THAT I CAN DO
    ECONOMICALLY SPEAKIN'
    I'M JUST WORKING FOR THE WEEKEND
    WHEN I HIT THE TOWN WITH YOU
    WHEN FRIDAY'S HERE IT'S VERY CLEAR
    MY FUTURE'S LOOKIN' BRIGHT
    'CAUSE I'M A MAN WITH A FINANCIAL PLAN
    I'M SAVING UP FOR SATURDAY NIGHT

    NOW I DON'T PLAY THE MARKET
    LIKE OTHER GUYS I KNOW
    MY TAB DOWN AT THE HONKY-TONK
    THAT'S MY PORTFOLIO
    I DON'T HAVE AN ACCOUNTANT
    BUT, BABY THAT'S ALRIGHT
    HE'D JUST SAY NOW CALL YOUR GIRL
    YOU CAN TAKE HER FOR A WHIRL
    'CAUSE YOU GOT JUST ENOUGH FOR SATURDAY NIGHT

    I'M SAVING UP FOR SATURDAY NIGHT
    THAT'S THE BEST THAT I CAN DO
    ECONOMICALLY SPEAKIN'
    I'M JUST WORKING FOR THE WEEKEND
    WHEN I HIT THE TOWN WITH YOU
    WHEN FRIDAY'S HERE IT'S VERY CLEAR
    MY FUTURE'S LOOKIN' BRIGHT
    I'M A MAN WITH A FINANCIAL PLAN
    I'M SAVING UP FOR SATURDAY NIGHT

ELDRIDGE. *(cont.)*

> FRIDAY'S HERE, IT'S VERY CLEAR
> MY FUTURE'S LOOKIN' BRIGHT
> AND IF I BLOW IT ALL,
> AT LEAST WE'LL HAVE A BALL,
> SAVING UP FOR SATURDAY NIGHT
>
> HELL, IF I BLOW IT ALL,
> AT LEAST WE'LL HAVE A BALL,
> SAVING UP FOR SATURDAY NIGHT

> *(**ELDRIDGE** takes a bow.)*

ELDRIDGE. Well, thank you, I appreciate that. *(to someone in the audience)* What's your name, darlin', where you in from?

> *(**ELDRIDGE** forgets he's doing a show and gets distracted with trying to get personal information from a gal in the audience.)*

ELDRIDGE. *(ad-lib flirts)* Are you stayin' over at the lodge? You got a king size or two doubles? No, it ain't part of my show, I just want to know. They give you an extra key? *(tries to close the deal)* All right, then we gotta work out a signal.

LUCINDA. Don't encourage him, darlin'. That's one stray you do not want followin' you home.

ELDRIDGE. Is that my Lucinda?

DOC. *(to **LUCINDA**)* Now you done it.

ELDRIDGE. I knew she couldn't stay mad at me a whole week.

LUCINDA. Oh, for the love o' Saint Criminy. Does he have to go and ruin my every weekend?

DOC. You knew he wasn't gonna stay in his dressing room all night.

LUCINDA. Then whoever he's got in the dressing room ain't doin' a very good job.

ELDRIDGE. If you're gonna accuse me of steppin' out on you, don't I at least get a hello kiss?

LUCINDA. Have you got no respect for a restraining order, Eldridge? That's close enough. You're supposed to keep at least a dance floor between us. So I don't strangle you.

DOC. It's for your own protection, El.

ELDRIDGE. This is still my place, Lucinda, and that fifty-foot perimeter swings both ways. If you gonna come in here, judge says I got a right to look but don't touch.

LUCINDA. Look yourself sticky, but you keep your hands on your half.

ELDRIDGE. And I decide which half's what and tonight the line goes from that jackalope in the corner over to the exit sign on your way out. So if you wanna stay, you gotta stay on that side, and I get over here.

LUCINDA. Fair enough.

ELDRIDGE. But if I happen to be sittin' on this barstool in the middle, I guess that means you got a legal right to give me a lap dance.

LUCINDA. The man has no shame. Eldridge Junior, where's your underpants?

ELDRIDGE. What makes you think I ain't wearing any?

LUCINDA. I was married to you, Eldridge. I know when your swagger's off.

DOC. Aw, El! She's right, you can't come out here like that. Where's your skivvies?

ELDRIDGE. *(changing the subject)* Hell, I dunno. Doc, have you seen Patsy with my coffee? We gotta get warmed up.

LUCINDA. You're not fooling anyone, El, she's back there with you. And the way you're dressed, I'd say she's plenty warm already.

DOC. Now go on, get changed. You're holdin' up the show.

(DOC ushers ELDRIDGE back to the dressing room.)

ELDRIDGE. All right, I'm goin', but I want her outta here by the time I get back.

DOC. She's a paying customer. You want her smack dab where she is until closing time.

ELDRIDGE. And keep her off my stage. This ain't your show no more, Lucinda. You tell her she's been replaced.

DOC. Go on tell her yourself.

ELDRIDGE. Are you lookin' to get me strangled?

DOC. Get back in your cage, El. *(calling backstage)* Patsy?

PATSY. *(offstage)* I'm not decent!

DOC. You don't have to be decent, just help him find his unmentionables.

LUCINDA. Not to mention yours! *(to DOC)* Is he really gonna let her in the show with him tonight? Girl's got talent.

DOC. She carries a tune.

LUCINDA. Wasn't talking about her singing.

DOC. Lucinda, get off the stage.

(**LUCINDA** *heads back to the bar)*

RODDY. You want I should vamp some more, Doc? I think I'm gettin' the hang of it.

DOC. Don't start with me, Roddy.

(**DOC** *heads back to the bar.* **RODDY** *vamps anyway.)*

*(MUSIC IN: **RODDY BACKGROUND**)*

DOC. *(to **LUCINDA**)* You ever thought about startin' trouble someplace else, for a change? Just for variety. I hear it's the spice.

LUCINDA. Would if I could, Doc. But there's not a lotta options in this one-honky-tonk town.

DOC. Well, just don't make me have to throw you out again. I only got the one good leg, and I think I pulled something last time you were here.

LUCINDA. That was your leg? Sorry, Doc, I thought you was gettin' fresh.

DOC. Do you want something from the bar? Or you just chattin' me up?

LUCINDA. Doc, I promise I'll be on my Sunday best behavior, tonight.

DOC. That'll be the day.

LUCINDA. You're right, I gotta stick with what I know. Roddy?

*(MUSIC IN: **LET ME SHOW YOU WHAT HE'S MISSING TONIGHT**)*

*(**LUCINDA** grabs a microphone, jumps up on the bar and sings one of her old numbers. **DOC** tries to get her down, but she stays out of his reach.)*

LUCINDA.

THERE'S A PHONE RINGING NOW
ON THE OTHER SIDE OF TOWN
THERE'S A MAN TRYING HARD TO GET THROUGH
LIKE A HUNDRED TIMES BEFORE
HE WANTS TO SAY HE'S SORRY NOW
BUT TONIGHT RINGIN'S ALL THAT PHONE'LL DO

SO LET ME SHOW YOU WHAT HE'S MISSING TONIGHT
LET ME SHOW YOU THE GOOD LOVE HE LEFT BEHIND
LET ME HOLD YOU IN MY ARMS GOOD AND TIGHT
AND I'LL SHOW YOU WHAT HE'S MISSING TONIGHT

THEY SAY A WOMAN SHOULD STAND BY HER MAN
WELL I'VE BEEN ON STANDBY WAY TOO LONG
THEY SAY A WOMAN SHOULD GIVE
ALL THE LOVE SHE CAN
WELL I KEPT GIVING 'TIL IT WAS ALL GONE

SO LET ME SHOW YOU WHAT HE'S MISSING TONIGHT
LET ME SHOW YOU THE GOOD LOVE HE LEFT BEHIND
LET ME HOLD YOU IN MY ARMS GOOD AND TIGHT
AND I'LL SHOW YOU WHAT HE'S MISSING TONIGHT

HE'LL APOLOGIZE FOR EACH AND EVERY LIE
HE'LL SAY HE MISSES WHAT WE SHARED
BUT DON'T YOU WORRY, HE'S JUST MISTAKEN ME
FOR SOMEONE WHO STILL CARES

LUCINDA. *(cont.)*

> LET ME SHOW YOU WHAT HE'S MISSING TONIGHT
> LET ME SHOW YOU THE GOOD LOVE HE LEFT BEHIND
> LET ME HOLD YOU IN MY ARMS GOOD AND TIGHT
> AND I'LL SHOW YOU WHAT HE'S MISSING TONIGHT
>
> YES, I'LL SHOW YOU WHAT HE'S MISSING TONIGHT

> *(**DOC** takes the microphone back from her.)*

DOC. I hope you got that outta your system.

LUCINDA. Oh, I dunno, Doc. My system's very complicated.

DOC. Slippery nipples?

LUCINDA. But you seem to know all my right buttons.

> *(**DOC** pours a couple of shots. They clink glasses. **LUCINDA** drinks hers. Then she drinks his. He was just holding it for her.)*

LUCINDA. Can I ask you something, Doc?

> *(MUSIC IN: **RODDY BACKGROUND**)*

DOC. You can ask, but you never listen. You want advice? Seek counseling.

LUCINDA. Nah, those headshrinkers charge by the hour, you only charge by the glass.

DOC. In that case, beer if it's your job, and whiskey everything else.

LUCINDA. Boilermaker it is.

> *(**DOC** makes her a drink.)*

> *(MUSIC IN: **WHATEVER'S LEFT OF ME**)*

> *(**RODDY** starts to sing…)*

RODDY.

> BABY, TIMES ARE HARD, EVERYBODY KNOWS IT…

> *(**DOC** cuts him off.)*

DOC. Roddy!

RODDY. What?

DOC. What'd I tell you about your singin' in mixed company?

RODDY. Not to go do it.

DOC. This is a public place. We got public people.

RODDY. She got to do one.

DOC. But she's not like to go singin' about her organs now, is she?

RODDY. Prob'ly not.

DOC. You do that on your own time.

RODDY. *(nods)* On my own time.

DOC. Patsy's gotta go on in a minute. You want her to have to follow that?

RODDY. I guess not.

DOC. You guessed right.

(**RODDY** *noodles innocuously.*)

(*MUSIC IN:* ***RODDY BACKGROUND***)

(**DOC** *returns to the bar.*)

LUCINDA. So, Doc, you gonna dance with me tonight?

DOC. There you go, makin' fun of the handicapped again. That's what gets you thrown outta places.

LUCINDA. Now, Doc, you ain't handicapped. And if I was making fun all this time, you'd prob'ly be fun by now.

DOC. You know I can't dance.

LUCINDA. I know you don't try.

DOC. I got at least two left feet that I know of–

LUCINDA. No, you got one left feet, and you're afraid to be seen hoppin'.

DOC. You do just fine without me holdin' you back.

LUCINDA. Don't say I didn't offer.

DOC. You always offer. I just know better 'n to believe you.

LUCINDA. Have a little faith, Doc. You gotta take a lady at her word now and again, if you wanna get your heart broke proper.

DOC. Now why would I want that?

LUCINDA. Because how you gonna know when the right girl comes along, if the wrong ones ain't done you no wrong?

DOC. I don't dance, Lucinda.

LUCINDA. Suit yourself. There's gotta be other fish in the sea. *(looking around)* I just wish we didn't live so far inland.

*(**ELDRIDGE** re-enters. He seems inexplicably more restrained.)*

ELDRIDGE. All right, are you satisfied?

LUCINDA. You and your undies don't satisfy me like they did back in high school, Eldridge.

ELDRIDGE. You say that now, but these are leopard print.

LUCINDA. You're about as romantic as a fold-out couch, you know that, El? And half as many useful positions.

ELDRIDGE. You want romance, you shoulda married your half-brother Tommy. Heh. That boy's romantic as a whole flower shop. If you know what I mean. Heh.

LUCINDA. Are you callin' him a pansy?

ELDRIDGE. If the petal fits... *(to audience)* Hello, everybody. Quite a crowd. What happened, another tour bus broke down on the interstate?

RODDY. Yeah, but we'll have that new axle for you first thing in the morning, folks.

ELDRIDGE. That was a hypo-torical question, Roddy.

RODDY. Ain't they all?

ELDRIDGE. *(to audience)* We got a great show for you–except for Roddy. That's Doc over at the bar, you prob'ly met. And I'm the man you've all been waiting for–

DOC. We did that part.

ELDRIDGE. Oh. Right. Okay, this next one's off my new album–

LUCINDA. You only got the one album. And it's at least ten years old.

ELDRIDGE. It's still the newest one! *(to audience)* But I see a lotta fellas out there dancin' in their seats. And that's hard on the upholstery. So let's make this one "ladies only" and see if that don't get 'em up. No pun intended, fellas. And ladies: pun intended.

*(MUSIC IN: **DANCE FLOOR DEMONS**)*

LUCINDA. There's my cue.

DOC. You ain't in the show.

LUCINDA. Doc, I am the show.

*(**LUCINDA** joins all the other gals on the dance floor.)*

ELDRIDGE.

WELL IN EVERY TOWN FROM TUPELO TO BATTLE CREEK
THERE'S A PLACE YOU GOTTA GO
AT THE END OF THE WEEK
IT'S A SATURDAY NIGHT
AND WORK IS FINALLY IS DONE
AND THERE'S A BUNCH OF GIRLS THERE
JUST TO HEAR THE BAND
THEY GOT A TABLE UP FRONT
JUST THE WAY THEY PLANNED
THE TIME IS RIGHT TO HAVE JUST A LITTLE FUN
WHEN THE MUSIC STARTS,
THEY CAN'T SIT DOWN NO MORE, NO!
AND THEY JUMP UP
AND BURN A HOLE RIGHT THROUGH THE FLOOR

THEY'RE THE DANCE FLOOR DEMONS OF THE USA
FROM CAROLINA CLEAR TO CALIFORN-I-A
THEY LOVE TO SHAKE IT UP
AND TAKE YOUR BREATH AWAY
THE DANCE FLOOR DEMONS OF THE USA

NOW IT HAS BEEN MY VERY VERY FORTUNATE FATE
TO STAND ON A STAGE IN NEARLY EVERY STATE
AND I CAN SAY ONE THING AND NOTHING ELSE IS TRUER
YEAH, WHEN THEY START TO ROCK
THEY'RE GONNA KNOCK YOU FLAT
TELL ME, HOW'D THEY EVER LEARN TO MOVE LIKE THAT?

ELDRIDGE. *(cont.)*
> AND EVERY GIRL IS FINER THAN THE ONE THAT'S RIGHT
>   NEXT TO HER
> AND IF I HAD ONE WISH I KNOW WHAT IT WOULD BE, YEAH!
> THAT THERE COULD BE ABOUT A MILLION OF ME
> ONE FOR EACH....
>
> DANCE FLOOR DEMON OF THE USA
> FROM CAROLINA CLEAR TO CALIFORN-I-A
> THEY LOVE TO SHAKE IT UP
> AND TAKE YOUR BREATH AWAY
> THE DANCE FLOOR DEMONS OF THE USA
>
> THEY'RE THE DANCE FLOOR DEMONS OF THE USA
> TRY TO HOLD THESE ANGELS BACK
> AND THERE'LL BE HELL TO PAY
> THEY LOVE TO SHAKE IT UP
> AND TAKE YOUR BREATH AWAY
> THE DANCE FLOOR DEMONS OF THE USA

> (**ELDRIDGE** *takes a bow.*)

ELDRIDGE. Thank you very much, Ladies. And Gentlemen: you're welcome. Say, Doc, can I get a little something up here to wet my whistle?

LUCINDA. If you're looking for Patsy, she's waitin' backstage. And she ain't that little.

ELDRIDGE. Now, Lucinda, that's no way to talk about the woman who's gonna be playing my wife.

LUCINDA. There's a thankless role.

ELDRIDGE. You see what I have to put up with, Doc?

DOC. Every Saturday.

LUCINDA. Doc?

DOC. I see what you put up with, too, Lucinda.

ELDRIDGE. What am I gonna do about her, Doc?

DOC. Usually, it's bourbon rocks with a cola back.

ELDRIDGE. Sounds about right. Roddy, would you go get that for me? I don't wanna cross no boundaries. *(to audience)* Now for this next number, I want to introduce you all… *(reads from a card)* to a little lady I hope you're gonna love just about as much as I do– But not quite as much, gentlemen, cuz I'm the jealous type. So let's have a lukewarm round of applause for… The girl of my dreams, the love of my life. The June Carter to my Cash. Heh heh. *(loses his place)* The…uh…

LUCINDA. Prettiest girl in the whole wide bar.

ELDRIDGE. Don't make me come over there, Lucinda.

LUCINDA. *(to* **DOC***)* He wrote that for me, y'know.

DOC. I wrote that for you. He just reads it off the cards.

ELDRIDGE. The prettiest girl in the whole wide bar. You know her, you love her, but I saw her first. My one and only one true love…Patsyyyyyyyyyyyyy… *(can't read the card)* Let's just call her Patsy.

*(MUSIC IN: **PATSY ENTRANCE FANFARE**)*

(Enter **PATSY***, in an outdated outfit that probably looked better on* **LUCINDA***.)*

PATSY. Hey, y'all, and welcome on out to the Honky Tonk Bar & Fill. My name is Patsy Dwindle, and I'll be your server tonight.

ELDRIDGE. Singer.

PATSY. Singer tonight. Specials are the pork tenderloin sandwich casserole – that comes with a side o' greens and a 2-dollar car wash – and we got a real nice center-cut steak and front end alignment–

ELDRIDGE. Patsy, you don't gotta do the specials. Just the singin' tonight.

PATSY. *(flustered)* I'm sorry, y'all, it's my first time up here, I'm a little nervous. I guess I just snapped back to what I know. Now, can I start you off with a drink or some antifreeze?

ELDRIDGE. Patsy, the song.

PATSY. Oh, right. I apologize, y'all. I'm messin' up awful, Eldridge.

LUCINDA. You're doing just fine, you little snake in the pants!

DOC. Lucinda, hush now.

PATSY. All right, everybody grab your partners–and your domestic partners–and let's see if we can't teach this ol' dance floor a thing or two–! *(almost forgot)* Oh, and make sure your car windows is rolled up, y'all, there's a storm coming in.

(*MUSIC IN: **NOW I'M SWINGIN'***)

LUCINDA. Whattaya say, Doc? Last chance.

DOC. I'm workin' here, Lucinda.

LUCINDA. That makes two of us.

(**LUCINDA** *grabs some other guy to dance with.*)

(*During* **PATSY***'s song,* **LUCINDA** *dances with every guy in the place. She pretty much steals the show.* **PATSY** *is steamed, but cheerfully tries not to show it till the song is over.*)

PATSY.

SOMETHING STRANGE IS COMING OVER ME
AND NOTHING IS THE WAY IT USED TO BE
YESTERDAY MY HEART WAS SAGGIN'
I WAS DRAGGING DOWN THE STREET
TODAY I FEEL LIKE BRAGGING
TO EVERYONE I MEET

NOTHING MUCH HAS CHANGED, NOW I SHOULD SAY
THE SUN CAME UP LIKE EVERY OTHER DAY
SO MAYBE IT'S THE WAY
YOU GOT ME DANCING LAST NIGHT
TO THAT MUSIC THEY WERE PLAYING,
THAT JUST FELT SO RIGHT

NOW I'M SWINGIN'
LIKE NO ONE'S EVER SWUNG BEFORE
FEEL LIKE SINGIN'
LIKE A BELL THAT'S NEVER RUNG BEFORE
IT'S JUST LIKE I HOPED LOVE WOULD BE
YOU CAME ALONG AND SUDDENLY
I'M FEELIN' WILD AND FREE...NOW I'M SWINGIN'

NOTHING MUCH HAS CHANGED, NOW I SHOULD SAY
THE SUN CAME UP LIKE EVERY OTHER DAY
SO MAYBE IT'S THE WAY
YOU GOT ME DANCING LAST NIGHT
TO THAT MUSIC THEY WERE PLAYING
FELT SO RIGHT

NOW I'M SWINGIN'
LIKE NO ONE'S EVER SWUNG BEFORE
FEEL LIKE SINGIN'
LIKE A BELL THAT'S NEVER RUNG BEFORE
IT'S JUST LIKE I HOPED LOVE WOULD BE
YOU CAME ALONG AND SUDDENLY
I'M WILD AND FREE...TAKE A LOOK AT ME

NOW I'M SWINGIN'
LIKE NO ONE'S EVER SWUNG BEFORE
FEEL LIKE SINGIN'
LIKE A BELL THAT'S NEVER RUNG BEFORE
IT'S JUST LIKE I HOPED LOVE WOULD BE
YOU CAME ALONG AND SUDDENLY
I'M FEELIN' WILD AND FREE...NOW I'M SWINGIN'

NOW I'M SWINGIN'

(After the song, **PATSY** *takes a bow.)*

PATSY. Thank you so much! You're all so sweet.

LUCINDA. *(to her partner)* Thank you, handsome. You just made the semi-finals. I'll announce a winner 'round about closing time. Must be present to win.

PATSY. Lucinda, can I have a word with you? *(takes her aside)* I know you don't like me, and you never have–

LUCINDA. And I never will—

PATSY. And I don't know why–

LUCINDA. And I'll give you a list: Dimwit... Talentless... Floozy...

PATSY. *(overlapping)* But it's my first night, and I'd appreciate if you don't steal all my thunder.

LUCINDA. That's my number and you know it. You're even wearin' my outfit.

PATSY. Used to be yours, Lucinda, when you and Eldridge was married and you did the show together. But now you're a divorcee. And Eldridge has given it to me. He's given it to me!

LUCINDA. What you two do in the privacy o' the back store room ain't none of my business, Patsy.

PATSY. Oh! You! She-witch!

*(**PATSY** attacks **LUCINDA**. Cat fight.)*

PATSY. You're just an ol' cougar! You know what that is?

LUCINDA. You know what a lobotomy is?

PATSY. Let go my hair!

LUCINDA. You let go!

DOC. All right, Lucinda. Girls! Don't make me limp over there.

ELDRIDGE. That's okay, Doc. I think I can handle this one.

*(**ELDRIDGE** merrily wades into the fray and separates them.)*

ELDRIDGE. Now quit! You know we got rules about weave-pullin'. You both oughta be ashamed of yourself, fussin' over a fella. Especially one that there's plenty of to go around. Am I right, Roddy?

RODDY. I'm not comfortable answering that, Eldridge.

ELDRIDGE. *(to **PATSY** and **LUCINDA**)* Now before I let you go, I think you both oughta owe me an apology.

LUCINDA. You??

PATSY. I'm sorry, Eldridge.

ELDRIDGE. Lucinda?

LUCINDA. It's not always all about you, Eldridge.

ELDRIDGE. Ha! That'll be the day.

LUCINDA. You're so full of yourself, you got rhinestones comin' out your ears, you know that? And I'm just sayin' "ears" to be polite.

(She tries to walk away.)

ELDRIDGE. You can turn your back, Lucinda, but it don't put me behind you.

LUCINDA. I don't even want to pretend to know what you think you're talkin' about.

ELDRIDGE. You want me to spell it out for you?

(**ELDRIDGE** *grabs the microphone, cues the band and sings at* **LUCINDA**.)

(*MUSIC IN:* ***TRYING TO GET OVER ME***)

ELDRIDGE.

> I SAW YOU WALKING DOWN THE STREET TODAY
> YOU HAD A SPRING IN YOUR STEP
> AND YOU WERE SMILING AWAY
> I KNOW YOU DON'T WANT ANYONE TO SEE
> THE PAIN YOU MUST BE GOING THROUGH
> TRYING TO GET OVER ME

> I KNOW YOU'RE FEELING ALL BROKE UP INSIDE
> THAT'S WHY YOU WENT OUT DANCING
> WITH THAT HANDSOME GUY
> PRETENDING YOU'RE NOT BLUE AS YOU MUST BE
> AND I KNOW YOU ONLY KISSED HIM,
> 'CAUSE YOU'RE TRYING TO GET OVER ME

> I WAS THE BEST THING YOU EVER HAD
> LIKE I TOLD YOU EVERY DAY
> AND NOW IT MAKES ME FEEL SO SAD
> YOU GOTTA MAKE BELIEVE THIS WAY
> WITH ALL THE HAPPINESS YOU'RE FAKING
> YOU CARRY ON COURAGEOUSLY
> WHILE YOUR POOR HEART IS BREAKING
> TRYING TO GET OVER ME

> SO KEEP YOUR CHIN UP NOW,
> IT AIN'T THE END OF THE WORLD
> YOU KNOW THAT YOU ARE STILL
> QUITE AN ATTRACTIVE GIRL
> I KNOW YOU'LL FIND SOMEONE EVENTUALLY
> NOW WHY YOU LAUGHING LIKE THAT?
> …YOU SHOULD BE TRYING TO GET OVER ME

ELDRIDGE. *(cont.)*

> I WAS THE BEST THING YOU EVER HAD
> LIKE I TOLD YOU EVERY DAY
> AND NOW IT MAKES ME FEEL SO SAD
> YOU GOTTA MAKE BELIEVE THIS WAY
> WITH ALL THE HAPPINESS YOU'RE FAKING
> YOU CARRY ON COURAGEOUSLY
> WHILE YOUR POOR HEART IS BREAKING
> TRYING TO GET OVER ME
>
> I KNOW THAT YOUR POOR HEART IS BREAKING
> TRYING TO GET OVER ME

LUCINDA. I ain't your problem no more, in case you think you forgot.

ELDRIDGE. Not till you come up in my business raisin' trouble.

LUCINDA. If it's more 'n you can handle, maybe you oughta have Doc call in the cops again.

DOC. I am not gonna do that.

ELDRIDGE. No, I think that's a good idea, Doc, you better call the police.

DOC. I'm not gonna do that, El.

LUCINDA. The only trouble you ever had was already in your pants when I got here.

PATSY. Who you calling "trouble?!"

DOC. Patsy, not now!

ELDRIDGE. You leave Patsy out of this.

LUCINDA. Nobody's talking about Patsy!

PATSY. Why not?!

DOC. Patsy, sit down!

PATSY. I'm a person, too!

ELDRIDGE. I didn't ask you to come here.

LUCINDA. Sure, you did. There's a big ol' sign right outside says: "Come on in!"

ELDRIDGE. There's also a sign that says: "This here's a respectable joint."

PATSY. And there's a picture of a marijuana leaf on it. It's kinda funny.

DOC. Patsy! Shush!

LUCINDA. Are you calling me irrespectable?

ELDRIDGE. If I thought I could pronounce it.

LUCINDA. You take that back!

ELDRIDGE. If you can't stand the heat...get the hell outta here!

DOC. Okay, that's enough. You both gotta settle down. *(separates them)* Now who's gonna be the bigger man?

LUCINDA. Oh, no! I ain't fallin' for that again. Make him be the man for once!

ELDRIDGE. This is a fine example you're setting for El-three. What's he gonna think, his momma comin' home in handcuffs and spandex? Again.

LUCINDA. This is pleather, you Neander-stine.

ELDRIDGE. And speaking of El-three, why aren't you home watchin' him? It's your weekend.

LUCINDA. It's always my weekend. You only get him on Tuesdays. Cuz you can't find the house any other day of the week.

ELDRIDGE. If you'd leave the damn porch light on!

LUCINDA. And you're one to talk, Eldridge. It took half your set to notice he was missing.

ELDRIDGE. Lucinda, what have you done with my boy?

LUCINDA. Don't get your chaps in a lather. He's fine. I got his Uncle Tommy watchin' him.

ELDRIDGE. His Uncle Tommy!? God-darn it, Lucinda, I asked you not to do that.

LUCINDA. There's nothing wrong with Tommy.

ELDRIDGE. Nothing a week in boot camp wouldn't fix. Unless it was Navy boot camp.

LUCINDA. Eldridge, that ain't even funny.

ELDRIDGE. The man is a powder-puff. He's a bad influence. You want our boy to grow up learning how to throw wrong?

LUCINDA. Tommy is the starting pitcher for the county softball team, for cryin' out loud. You're the only one in this family throws like a musician. *(to the band)* No offense, Roddy.

RODDY. No, ma'am.

LUCINDA. If you're worried about El-three pickin' up a fashion sense and a decent curve ball, you might wanna pony up for some day care.

ELDRIDGE. That's blackmail!

LUCINDA. No, it's child support, you jackass. And you're behind again, so I got relatives watchin' him. And if that don't sit right with you, better grab yourself a cushion seat and get used to sittin' wrong.

ELDRIDGE. We'll see how wrong I sit after I get through with him!

LUCINDA. Where are you going?

ELDRIDGE. I'm gonna rescue my boy outta there before I have to explain to him about the birds and the birds.

LUCINDA. Don't you go over there, Eldridge.

ELDRIDGE. Or what? You'll make my life even more of a living heck than it already is because of you? Well, get in line! Behind yourself! Then kiss my behind. Which'll be two in front of you.

LUCINDA. I didn't make your life anything it wasn't already trainwrecked out to be when I met you.

ELDRIDGE. I wouldn't be here in this gosh-forsaken podunk of a town—no offense, folks—if it wasn't for you!

LUCINDA. You was born here, Eldridge.

ELDRIDGE. But you're the one stuck us here.

LUCINDA. Me?!

ELDRIDGE. If I hadn't hooked up with you at the high school dance, I woulda been hell up and gone the day after graduation.

LUCINDA. So now it was a hook up?! That senior prom was the happiest day of your life, and don't you forget it.

ELDRIDGE. I thought our wedding was supposed to be the happiest day.

LUCINDA. The wedding was nice, too, but there was a lot less screaming at the prom.

ELDRIDGE. I coulda gone places, Lucinda. If you'da been worth the trip.

LUCINDA. What's that supposed to mean?

ELDRIDGE. *(cruelly)* You used to be somethin'.

LUCINDA. I'm still somethin'!

ELDRIDGE. Yeah. But I hear they got a cream for that now.

LUCINDA. What?!

ELDRIDGE. Doc, keep an eye on her for me. While I'm gone, she don't go past this barstool. Patsy, I don't wanna hear nothin' but ballads till I get back. Roddy!

RODDY. Vamp?

ELDRIDGE. The fun has left the building!

(**ELDRIDGE** *leaves the building*).

DOC. El Jay, come back here. You got a show to do.

(**DOC** *limps off after him.*)

LUCINDA. I'm still something!

(**PATSY** *hurries onto the stage in another of Lucinda's old outfits.*)

PATSY. *(to audience)* Well, that was a sight more excitement than I was hoping for on my first night. So I guess we're gonna slow things up a notch. You folks need to simmer some. Two notches for you, mister. *(interrupts herself)* Y'all, I wanna apologize if I about hurt somebody a minute ago. I probably shouldn'ta been tusslin'…

(*MUSIC IN:* ***SHE WANTED TO BE A SINGER***)

PATSY.
> SHE GETS UP EVERY MORNING
> AN HOUR BEFORE THE DAWN
> AND MAKES HER CUP OF COFFEE
> AND WAKES HER LITTLE ONE
> IT'S TIME FOR SCHOOL,

PATSY. *(cont.)*

SO SHE SENDS HIM ON HIS WAY
TIME TO FACE THE WORLD,
SHE'S GOT BILLS TO PAY

SHE ONCE HAD A YOUNG MAN,
SO LONG AGO IT SEEMS
IN SECRET LOVERS' WHISPERS
THEY SHARED THEIR SPECIAL DREAMS
NOW SHE'S ALONE WITH THE CHILD HE LEFT BEHIND
ON HER OWN, AND SHE REALLY WOULDN'T MIND...

BUT SHE WANTED TO BE A SINGER
AND GET A PIECE OF THE BRIGHT SPOT LIGHT
SHE WANTED BE A SINGER
SENDING SONGS OUT INTO THE NIGHT
AND SHE DREAMS OF THE JOY IT WOULD BRING HER
IF SHE HAD A CHANCE TO PLAY
SHE WANTED TO BE A SINGER
BUT LIFE GOT IN THE WAY

*(**DOC** comes back in. He sees **LUCINDA** sitting at the bar, looking more hurt than she wants to admit.)*

PATSY.

THE RADIO'S HER BEST FRIEND,
SHE KNOWS ALL OF THE SONGS
AND DEEP INSIDE SHE WONDERS
IF A CHANCE MIGHT COME ALONG
AND LATE AT NIGHT
WHEN THEY BOTH HAVE SLEEPY EYES
SHE HOLDS HIM TIGHT AND SINGS HIM LULLABIES

SHE WANTED TO BE A SINGER
AND GET A PIECE OF THE BRIGHT SPOT LIGHT
SHE WANTED BE A SINGER
NOTHING ELSE COULD FEEL AS RIGHT
AND SHE DREAMS OF THE JOY IT WOULD BRING HER
IF SHE HAD A CHANCE TO PLAY
SHE WANTED TO BE A SINGER
BUT LIFE GOT IN THE WAY

SHE WANTED TO BE A SINGER
BUT LIFE GOT IN THE WAY...

Thank you all. You've been real sweet. So I hope you saved room for dessert. We got some extra-good home-mades. I know I'm gonna have the chocolate brownie fudge cake and a good cry.

(**PATSY** *runs offstage.*)

LUCINDA. *(to* **DOC***)* He's right you know.

DOC. Eldridge ain't never been right about nothing didn't have answers on the box top.

LUCINDA. You tried to warn us at the wedding. You remember?

DOC. That wasn't a warning, it was a toast. It was supposed to be funny.

LUCINDA. You got a grim sense of humor for a best man.

DOC. I said I was sorry.

LUCINDA. What'd you have to be sorry about? We was the one's "throwin' away our last chance at happiness."

DOC. Your folks laughed.

LUCINDA. Why the hell do I keep comin' here, week after week?

DOC. Well, you know what they say about old habits, and how many times you gotta back over 'em.

LUCINDA. The Dew Drop's just another half-mile down the road. I could walk it in a low heel.

DOC. You're not gonna do that. You'd miss it too much. Saturday nights at the ol' Bar & Fill. I know you miss being up on that stage, and out on the dance floor.

LUCINDA. You're right, the Dew Drop's got a lousy juke box.

DOC. Not to mention, I like to think, you'd miss the spar-kling conversation that keeps you coming back for more.

(**RODDY** *noodles.*)

(*MUSIC IN:* ***RODDY BACKGROUND***)

LUCINDA. You and me go back a long way, Doc.

DOC. Since high school.

LUCINDA. How come I didn't end up with more of a guy like you?

DOC. Are you askin' for serious?

LUCINDA. No, I'm gunnin' for a free drink.

DOC. Well, probably cuz you and Eldridge hit it off at the senior prom. And at the time it was all the little girl dreams you thought you needed to come true.

LUCINDA. Are you sayin' I grew up?

DOC. Grew up. Stopped dreaming. Same difference.

(**DOC** *pours* **LUCINDA** *another drink.*)*

*(MUSIC IN: **WHATEVER'S LEFT OF ME**)*

RODDY.

BABY, TIMES ARE HARD, EVERYBODY KNOWS IT...

LUCINDA. Roddy!

RODDY. What?

LUCINDA. Aren't you on a break?

RODDY. Doc said I could play on my own time.

LUCINDA. Yeah, and when you get your own bar. This ain't that kinda place.

DOC. Customer's always right, Roddy.

RODDY. Kinda mean, too.

LUCINDA. *(to* **DOC***)* You ever think about what coulda been? If things had turned out different?

DOC. How do you mean?

LUCINDA. We were all at that same prom.

DOC. Not me. I was still on crutches from the time Eldridge ran my Jeep into that bridge.

LUCINDA. That's right. He wrecked you up pretty good. And your Jeep.

DOC. I never was much for school dances, but that pretty much cinched it for me.

---

*See Appendix 1 for optional song.

LUCINDA. That's what I mean, though. If you'da been driving instead o' the passenger seat? What mighta been? Maybe you'd be the star o' the show, and he'd be Doc the cripple bartender.

DOC. Maybe I'da stayed on the road and we wouldn't be havin' this conversation.

LUCINDA. If El hadn't been the only fella asked me to dance that night, who knows whose first wife I'd be right now. Instead I'm the washed-up ex of a washout son of a car wash entrepreneur. And you limp around his daddy's bar writing songs for us to sing at each other. And we don't even do that anymore.

DOC. Could be worse. It could be raining.

PATSY. *(runs through)* It's coming down, y'all!

LUCINDA. Where did we go wrong, Doc?

DOC. We? How'd I get drug into this?

LUCINDA. Well, look at us. We're both here every single weekend. We're both going home single tonight.

DOC. There's one easy way to fix that for both of us.

LUCINDA. Is it last call already? You're hittin' on me kinda early tonight.

DOC. Not my fault you're lookin' desperate ahead o' schedule.

LUCINDA. You keep comin' on sweet, all it's gonna get you is cavities.

DOC. You keep tellin' me "no," it's how I know you're okay to drive.

*(MUSIC IN: **LET'S DO SOMETHING CHEAP AND SUPERFICIAL**)*

*(**DOC** hits on **LUCINDA** like he does every Saturday.)*

DOC.

I'VE BEEN LOOKING IN YOUR BLOODSHOT EYES
THROUGH THIS SMOKY BARROOM HAZE
AND LISTENING TO THE TRAGEDIES
OF ALL YOUR YESTERDAYS

DOC. *(cont.)*

LIKE THE NO GOOD GUY WHO LEFT YOU
AND YOUR KID AND ALL THE REST
WELL NOW IT'S GETTING KIND OF LATE
AND I HAVE ONE SMALL REQUEST

ALTHOUGH YOUR HAIR IS ALL IN TANGLES
AND YOUR MAKEUP IS A MESS
AND MOST OF WHAT YOU'RE DRINKING
IS SPILLING DOWN YOUR DRESS
AND TO KEEP FROM FALLING OFF YOUR BARSTOOL'S
'BOUT ALL THAT YOU CAN DO
I'LL MAKE MY PROPOSITION
'CAUSE I'M JUST 'BOUT AS DRUNK AS YOU

LET'S DO SOMETHING CHEAP AND SUPERFICIAL
LET'S DO SOMETHING THAT WE MIGHT REGRET
LET'S DO SOMETHING SHABBY AND INSENSITIVE
'CAUSE THIS MIGHT BE THE ONLY CHANCE WE GET

YOU'VE GOT LIPSTICK SHOWING ON YOUR TEETH
AND A RUN DOWN YOUR HOSE
AND WHERE YOU GOT THAT CHEAP PERFUME
WELL, GOD ONLY KNOWS
NOW I'LL BE GLAD TO HAVE YOU HOME
LONG BEFORE DAYLIGHT
THE SUN IS YOUR WORST ENEMY
SO I'M GLAD IT'S DARK TONIGHT

DOC.	**LUCINDA.**
LET'S DO SOMETHING	
CHEAP AND	
SUPERFICIAL	SUPERFICIAL
LET'S DO SOMETHING	
THAT WE MIGHT	
REGRET	MIGHT REGRET
LET'S DO SOMETHING	
SHABBY AND	
INSENSITIVE	INSENSITIVE

DOC.

'CAUSE THIS MIGHT BE THE ONLY CHANCE WE GET
YEAH, THIS MIGHT BE THE ONLY CHANCE WE GET

LUCINDA. You're just lucky I know you don't mean it.

DOC. You gotta take a fella at his word now and then, if you wanna get your heart broke proper.

LUCINDA. Yeah, all right.

DOC. What's all right?

LUCINDA. This.

(**LUCINDA** *kisses him.*)

DOC. *(to audience)* Last call!

(**DOC** *grabs* **LUCINDA** *and heads for the back room.*)

PATSY. What? Doc? Where you going?

DOC. You don't have to go home, but you can't stay here!

(**DOC** *and* **LUCINDA** *duck out.*)

PATSY. No, wait! Nobody leave. You can stay here. You don't have to go home. Doc? Eldridge? *(beat)* Roddy?

RODDY. Yeah?

PATSY. I think one of us just got a promotion...

(*MUSIC IN:* ***WHATEVER'S LEFT OF ME***)

RODDY.
BABY, TIMES ARE HARD–

PATSY. Roddy! Don't start with me!

RODDY. Sorry, boss.

PATSY. *(to the audience)* Don't mind Roddy, folks. We just keep him around for the desserts.

RODDY. Try the carrot cake!

PATSY. And Roddy's apple pie is better than McDonald's.

RODDY. The secret is carrots.

PATSY. Don't you got a kitchen to explode?

RODDY. I'm on it.

(**RODDY** *exits.*)

PATSY. So I guess we're gonna take a little break here, so why don't y'all just—?

(*explosion in the kitchen*)

PATSY. *(sheepishly)* I better get that. Enjoy your intermission.

(**PATSY** *exits.*)

END OF ACT I

ACT II

(Later that night. **PATSY** *pounds on the door to the dressing room.)*

PATSY. Doc, it's almost showtime! Doc? *(hesitates to ask)* Lucinda?

*(***LUCINDA*** *pokes her head out of the dressing room.)*

LUCINDA. We was kinda hoping for some privacy.

PATSY. Eldridge ain't back yet, and the break's about over.

*(***DOC*** *pokes his head out of the dressing room.)*

DOC. He's not back?! Why the–? *(beat)* Why are you covered in chocolate?

PATSY. You prob'ly don't wanna know.

DOC. You're prob'ly right. Sorry I asked.

PATSY. Apology accepted.

DOC. Just go get ready to sing. Where's Roddy?

PATSY. You said you don't want to know.

DOC. Just go.

*(***PATSY*** *exits, leaving* ***DOC*** *and* ***LUCINDA*** *alone again. Awkward silence.)*

LUCINDA. So I guess I'll see you next week?

DOC. You're not leaving, are you?

LUCINDA. Well, the way I figure it, you gotta work, and I got a kid. With the guy you work for. Who's prob'ly on his way back here right now. And prob'ly wouldn't understand.

DOC. Prob'ly not.

(uncomfortable silence)

DOC. Y'know, there's no reason this has to be awkward.

(**RODDY** *enters, sheepishly, covered in chocolate, and slinks back to his place.*)

LUCINDA. Sure, it does, Doc.

DOC. I know. I was just making conversation.

(**LUCINDA** *turns to go*).

DOC. Lucinda, wait. You and me, we've been friends for too long for this to have to change everything.

LUCINDA. I know. But it ain't really up to us, is it?

DOC. How do you mean?

LUCINDA. C'mon, Doc, the town ain't that big. Somehow I don't see keeping what just happened between us… *(cocks her head toward the audience)* just between us.

*(MUSIC IN: **SMALL TOWN**)*

DOC. Yeah… Folks don't make it easy.

(sings)

I'LL SEE YOU ON THE STREET

LUCINDA.

WE'LL SMILE AND SAY HELLO

DOC.

WE'LL TALK ABOUT THE WEATHER

LUCINDA.

WILL IT RAIN?

DOC.

WELL, I DON'T KNOW
THEN WE'LL WALK AWAY BEFORE WE SAY

LUCINDA.

WHAT'S REALLY ON OUR MINDS

DOC.

THERE'S A HUNDRED EARS
THAT WOULD LOVE TO HEAR
WHERE WE'RE GONNA BE TONIGHT…..

LUCINDA & DOC.

'CAUSE IT'S A SMALL TOWN AND PEOPLE TALK
NEWS TRAVELS FAST UP AND DOWN THE BLOCK
AND WHAT GOES ON WHEN THE SUN GOES DOWN

LUCINDA.
AIN'T NOBODY'S BUSINESS
DOC.
'TIL IT GETS AROUND
LUCINDA & DOC.
YES IT'S A SMALL TOWN, AND DON'T YOU DOUBT IT
STEP OUT OF LINE AND THEY'LL FIND OUT ABOUT IT
DOC.
TONIGHT WE'LL SHARE THE SECRET LOVE WE FOUND
LUCINDA.
'TIL THEN WE'LL PRETEND WE'RE JUST FRIENDS
LUCINDA & DOC.
'CAUSE HONEY, IT'S A SMALL TOWN
DOC.
WELL, THERE'S A SPY ON EVERY CORNER
AND EVERYONE KNOWS EVERYONE
LUCINDA.
AND IF YOU'VE GOT A SECRET
IT'S HARD TO KEEP IT VERY LONG
DOC.
SO WE WON'T TAKE NO CHANCES
WHEN WE MEET IN THE LIGHT OF DAY
LUCINDA.
NO LONG AND LOVING GLANCES
THAT COULD GIVE IT ALL AWAY....
LUCINDA & DOC.
'CAUSE IT'S A SMALL TOWN AND PEOPLE TALK
NEWS TRAVELS FAST UP AND DOWN THE BLOCK
AND WHAT GOES ON WHEN THE SUN GOES DOWN
LUCINDA.
AIN'T NOBODY'S BUSINESS
DOC.
'TIL IT GETS AROUND
LUCINDA & DOC.
YES IT'S A SMALL TOWN, AND DON'T YOU DOUBT IT
STEP OUT OF LINE AND THEY'LL FIND OUT ABOUT IT

DOC.
TONIGHT WE'LL SHARE THE SECRET LOVE WE FOUND
LUCINDA.
'TIL THEN WE'LL PRETEND WE'RE JUST FRIENDS
LUCINDA & DOC.
'CAUSE HONEY, IT'S A SMALL TOWN
IT'S A SMALL TOWN
IT'S A SMALL TOWN

(awkward silence)

DOC. I didn't mean for this to happen.

LUCINDA. Thanks. It was good for me, too.

DOC. That's not what I meant.

LUCINDA. I know what you meant.

DOC. He's my best friend…

LUCINDA. I know.

DOC. He's your husband…

LUCINDA. Ex-husband.

DOC. I'm not sayin' we can't–

LUCINDA. I know you're not.

DOC. But it's like you said. It's not really up to us.

LUCINDA. So it's all about Eldridge. He'd like that.

DOC. No, he would not.

LUCINDA. I know. I was just making conversation.

*(**PATSY** rushes in with a kitchen sponge.)*

PATSY. He's back! It's Eldridge! Everybody act natural.

*(Everybody but **PATSY** was already acting natural. **PATSY** gives **RODDY** a quick wipe down, then tries to act natural.)*

*(**ELDRIDGE** staggers in. He has a big black eye.)*

ELDRIDGE. *(glares at **LUCINDA**)* There she is!

LUCINDA. Here we go.

ELDRIDGE. Well, I hope you're happy.

LUCINDA. There's a first time for everything.

DOC. Eldridge! Where have you been? And why are you soaking wet?

ELDRIDGE. It's pouring down cats and dogs out there, in case you didn't notice. Be nice if we let people know about that before they go leave their convertible outside with the top down.

LUCINDA. El, what happened to your eye?

ELDRIDGE. You know perfectly well what happened!

LUCINDA. *(grins)* Yeah, but I want to hear you tell it.

ELDRIDGE. Your son's Uncle Tommy's what happened. The man is a powder keg. He's a bad influence.

LUCINDA. I told you not to go over there.

DOC. We gotta get something on that eye. Patsy, get him a steak.

PATSY. How would you like that prepared?

DOC. For his eye, Patsy. Hurry up! He's gotta go on in a minute.

LUCINDA. So where's El-three?

ELDRIDGE. He's fine.

LUCINDA. Nuh uh. That's not an answer. What've you done with my baby?

ELDRIDGE. Don't get your panties in a gather. I said he's fine. I got his Uncle Tommy watchin' him.

LUCINDA. My half-brother Tommy Uncle Tommy?!

ELDRIDGE. You want our boy to grow up knowing how to throw a decent punch?

LUCINDA. You're unbelievable, you know that?

ELDRIDGE. You wouldn't believe me if I was believable.

LUCINDA. So now that he's violent, Tommy's okay by you?

ELDRIDGE. What do you want me to do? Admit I was wrong? Is that what you want?

LUCINDA. Yes, that's what I want.

ELDRIDGE. Then why don't you just come out and say it? Why we gotta play all these mind games all the time trying to trick me into saying what we both know you won't admit is what you was trying to get me to do all along?

LUCINDA. What just happened in your brain? Is that supposed to be an apology? Cuz I think you missed a spot.

ELDRIDGE. *(to* DOC*)* You see how she is?

DOC. *(changing the subject)* Well, I'm glad that's settled. Now, are you gonna get ready?

ELDRIDGE. Calm down, Doc, I told you, I was born that way. *(to* **LUCINDA***)* You want an apology? I'll give you an apology.

(**ELDRIDGE** *grabs the microphone.*)

ELDRIDGE. Folks, I want to dedicate this next number to the girl who keeps on breaking my heart. Every week like clockwork.

LUCINDA. That ain't gonna work, Eldridge.

ELDRIDGE. Why don't you come on up here, Lucinda?

DOC. Leave her be, El.

ELDRIDGE. Hit it, Roddy. *(to* **LUCINDA***)* C'mon, baby. Just one song. You and me. For old times? No? How about for next month's child support?

LUCINDA. You're playin' with dynamite, El.

ELDRIDGE. I knew that when I married you.

LUCINDA. I don't have to listen to this…

ELDRIDGE. Roddy, what part of "hit it," do you need on a flashcard?

*(MUSIC IN: **COME ON, LUCINDA**)*

(**ELDRIDGE** *tries to get* **LUCINDA** *to dance with him, but she sits at the bar and refuses. So* **ELDRIDGE** *ends up dancing with all the other girls. Eventually,* **LUCINDA** *gets up and walks out.)*

ELDRIDGE.

WELL FROM THE MOMENT YOU WALKED IN I'VE HAD MY
EYE ON YOU
AND UNLESS I MISS MY GUESS, WELL YOU'VE BEEN LOOKING
AT ME, TOO
WELL WE COULD KEEP ON GLANCIN' THE WHOLE NIGHT
THROUGH
YEAH, BUT I CAME FOR DANCIN', GIRL, NOW HOW 'BOUT
YOU?

NOW IF I WALK RIGHT OVER AND SAY HELLO
ARE YOU GONNA GIVE ME A SMILE?
NOW YOU COULD CHANGE MY WORLD FOREVER TONIGHT
YOU KNOW
AT LEAST FOR A LITTLE WHILE

COME ON LUCINDA,
YOU GOTTA GET UP AND DANCE
COME ON LUCINDA,
YOU KNOW YOU REALLY OUGHTA TAKE A LITTLE CHANCE

SITTING OVER THERE
IN THAT NAUGAHYDE CHAIR
NOW THAT AIN'T WHERE YOU WANT TO BE
SO COME ON LUCINDA, COME ON LUCINDA
LUCY COME AND DANCE WITH ME

WHY DON'T YOU TELL ME THE NAME OF YOUR FAVORITE
SONG?
I'LL GIVE THE BAND A TWENTY AND THEY'LL PLAY IT
PLENTY LONG
I'M NOT A LOT TO LOOK AT BUT I GUARANTEE
NO ONE'S EVER GONNA TREAT YOU HALF AS GOOD AS ME

YOU NEVER KNOW WHERE THIS COULD GO, YOU JUST
MIGHT
SWEAR FOREVER TO BE MINE
BUT I'M NOT REALLY ASKING FOR YOUR HAND TONIGHT
YOU GOT TWO GOOD FEET AND THAT'LL DO JUST FINE

ELDRIDGE. *(cont.)*

> COME ON LUCINDA,
> YOU GOTTA GET UP AND DANCE
> COME ON LUCINDA,
> YOU KNOW YOU REALLY OUGHTA TAKE A LITTLE CHANCE
>
> SITTING OVER THERE
> IN THAT NAUGAHYDE CHAIR
> THAT AIN'T WHERE YOU WANT TO BE
> SO COME ON LUCINDA, COME ON LUCINDA
> LUCY COME AND DANCE WITH ME
>
> WELL COME ON LUCINDA,
> YOU GOTTA GET UP AND DANCE
> COME ON LUCINDA,
> YOU KNOW YOU REALLY OUGHTA TAKE A LITTLE CHANCE
>
> PUT DOWN THAT LITTLE PINK DRINK, WHATEVER IT IS
> IN MY ARMS IS WHERE YOU WANT TO BE
> SO COME ON LUCINDA, COME ON LUCINDA
> LUCY COME AND DANCE WITH ME
>
> YEAH, COME ON LUCINDA, COME ON LUCINDA
> LUCY COME AND DANCE WITH ME

*(***ELDRIDGE*** *looks around the room, but* **LUCINDA** *is gone.)*

ELDRIDGE. Where's Lucinda?

DOC. She's gone.

ELDRIDGE. *(bellows, distraught)* Nooo!! She can't be gone! I can't lose her again! Not like this.

DOC. She's gone to the bathroom, El. She'll be right back.

ELDRIDGE. Oh.

DOC. She got tired o' hearin' you go on about her.

ELDRIDGE. Well, don't scare me like that, Doc. I thought I lost her for good this time.

DOC. I think that kite has sailed, El. You lost her the day the divorce went final.

ELDRIDGE. Don't you think I know that?! *(getting paranoid)* But tonight something's different. Something's changed. Even after she left me, Lucinda always come in here every Saturday to hear me play.

DOC. She still does, El. She's here right now. Just like always.

ELDRIDGE. I think there's someone else. Another man. I know it. I can feel him.

DOC. You're imagining things.

ELDRIDGE. Then how come she's got a spring in her step I ain't seen since high school?

DOC. She does?

ELDRIDGE. You didn't notice? She's been cattin' around like a school kitten all night long.

DOC. She has?

ELDRIDGE. It's gotta be one of these new fellas in from off that tour bus. *(eyes the audience suspiciously)* I don't know which one it is. But he's watching me right now. I can feel him ooglin' me. Like his eyes keep following me everywhere I go.

*(***ELDRIDGE*** zigs and zags. **DOC** watches him.)*

ELDRIDGE. *(accuses the audience in general…)* Don't think I don't know what you think you're up to! *(…and one guy in particular)* Or you, if it's you. *(to* **DOC***)* Did you see that? He flinched. *(to guy)* You flinched! *(to* **DOC***)* That's a guilty flinch if ever I saw one.

DOC. All right, stop it, El. You're just making yourself crazy.

ELDRIDGE. I bet that's just what he wants me to make!!

*(***DOC*** steers **ELDRIDGE** away from the audience.)*

DOC. Now, sit down, you're scarin' the customers. Have a drink.

ELDRIDGE. What am I gonna do, Doc?!

DOC. Shot o' tequila.

ELDRIDGE. Doc, I'm serious. I need your help.

DOC. I'll tell you the same thing I told you both at the wedding. You might wanna knock off this nonsense and get on with your lives before you do something you're both gonna regret, and the rest of us have to watch.

ELDRIDGE. *(laughing)* You were the funniest best man ever.

DOC. This ain't a joke no more, Eldridge. You're not doing anybody any good draggin' things out.

ELDRIDGE. *(maudlin)* She's the girl of my dreams. The love of my life. The prettiest girl in the whole wide bar.

DOC. That was real touchin', El. When I wrote it.

ELDRIDGE. I thought you were my friend!

DOC. And the tequila's on me.

ELDRIDGE. What kinda best man don't help his best friend's girl from runnin' off on him? You think just cuz I'm shallow, my feelings don't get hurt? I also happen to be thin-skinned!

DOC. And thick-headed.

ELDRIDGE. There you go. I'm too stupid to change!

DOC. You're too stupid to live, but that don't stop you.

ELDRIDGE. If she ever left me for real and for good, I don't know what I'd do. But I'm pretty sure I wouldn't like it. Do you know what that's like? Wantin' something so bad that you'd ruin both your lives just to keep her in yours?

(**DOC** *knows.*)

DOC. You ever thought about telling her that?

ELDRIDGE. Are you kidding, Doc? Why do you think I married her? So we don't have to get into that.

DOC. Well, maybe that's what it's gonna take.

ELDRIDGE. She's the best thing ever happened to me, and the worst. And half the time I can't tell which is which. So I want 'em both. What's wrong with me, Doc? And don't tell me it's me, cuz I ain't hearin' it.

DOC. It's you.

ELDRIDGE. Dang it, I knew it.

(*MUSIC IN:* ***IF YOU DON'T TELL HER***)

(**DOC** *pours* **ELDRIDGE** *another round and offers him the only advice he can.*)

DOC.

> I KNOW HOW YOU FEEL ABOUT HER
> IT COMES AS NO SURPRISE
> SINCE THE FIRST TIME THAT YOU SAW HER
> I COULD SEE IT IN YOUR EYES
> NOW I'M JUST GIVING YOU A CLUE
> SO LET ME TELL YOU AS A FRIEND
> YOU BETTER LET HER KNOW 'CAUSE YOU
> JUST MIGHT NOT GET THIS SHOT AGAIN
>
> IF YOU DON'T TELL HER THAT YOU LOVE HER
> YOUR GONNA LOSE HER FAST
> IF YOU DON'T TELL HER THAT YOU LOVE HER
> THIS CHANCE COULD BE YOUR LAST
> IF YOU WAIT TOO MUCH LONGER
> SHE MIGHT NOT BE THERE STILL
> 'CAUSE IF YOU DON'T TELL HER THAT YOU LOVE HER
> I KNOW SOMEONE WHO WILL

ELDRIDGE. She's my everything. And she don't want nothing to do with me.

DOC.

> WE BOTH CAN SEE SHE'S THE KIND OF GIRL
> YOU DON'T FIND EVERY DAY
> AND SOME GUYS WOULD BE GLAD
> TO LET YOU LET HER SLIP AWAY
> BUT ME AND YOU GO BACK A WHILE
> SO I'VE GIVEN THIS SOME THOUGHT
> YOU SHOULD TAKE THE TIME TO TELL HER NOW
> 'CAUSE BOY THAT'S ALL THE TIME YOU'VE GOT
>
> IF YOU DON'T TELL HER THAT YOU LOVE HER
> YOUR GONNA LOSE HER FAST
> IF YOU DON'T TELL HER THAT YOU LOVE HER
> THIS CHANCE COULD BE YOUR LAST
> IF YOU WAIT TOO MUCH LONGER
> SHE MIGHT NOT BE THERE STILL
> 'CAUSE IF YOU DON'T TELL HER THAT YOU LOVE HER
> I KNOW SOMEONE WHO WILL

DOC. *(cont.)*

> YEAH, THERE IS SOMETHING ABOUT HER
> THAT DOES SOMETHING TO A MAN
> AND YOU DON'T WANT TO LIVE WITHOUT HER
> NOW I CAN REALLY UNDERSTAND
>
> BUT THIS WORLD IS FULL OF SECRETS
> AND ONE OF THEM MIGHT SPILL
> 'CAUSE IF YOU DON'T TELL HER THAT YOU LOVE HER
> I THINK I KNOW SOMEONE WHO WILL
> I KNOW SOMEONE WHO WILL
> I KNOW SOMEONE WHO WILL
>
> *(**LUCINDA** comes back in. They both stare at her.)*

LUCINDA. You're outta paper towels. *(beat)* Why is everybody lookin' at me?

DOC. *(prompting him)* El?

ELDRIDGE. *(clueless)* What?

DOC. *(prompting again)* Lucinda, Eldridge has something he wants to say to you.

ELDRIDGE. No, I don't.

DOC. What did we just talk about?!

ELDRIDGE. Oh, right. Lucinda, I got something I wanna say to you.

LUCINDA. Stay on your half.

ELDRIDGE. Lucinda, baby…Honey…Sugar Pie…You and me… Well, we been through a lot.

LUCINDA. Yeah, I was there for the proceedings.

ELDRIDGE. *(turning to **DOC**)* I can't do this, if she's gonna be like that.

DOC. Get back over there!

ELDRIDGE. Lucinda…

LUCINDA. Baby, Honey, Sugar Pie–Yeah, we done this part.

ELDRIDGE. You know how I feel about you…

LUCINDA. I know how you act around me.

ELDRIDGE. Well, there you go. And actions is louder than words. So you oughta know by now my actions been screamin' their head off since you divorced me.

LUCINDA. We both divorced each other.

ELDRIDGE. You started it!

LUCINDA. Can I get a drink? I'm gonna need something to throw in his face.

(**PATSY** *enters with a grilled steak.*)

PATSY. What's going on? What's he doing? Is he proposing to her?

DOC. I hope not. He's already got the one black eye.

ELDRIDGE. Lucinda, I never said this to any woman alive before. Except my dog Duchess. And she's dead. So she don't count.

LUCINDA. She's a dog is why she don't count.

ELDRIDGE. You best not be bad-mouthing my dog.

LUCINDA. You just don't know when to quit, do you?

ELDRIDGE. Well, what do you expect from me??

LUCINDA. About like this, don't get me wrong.

ELDRIDGE. Well, dammit, Lucinda!

LUCINDA. Don't you got a show to do?

ELDRIDGE. Forget about the show, Lucinda! Don't you know there's more important things in life??

LUCINDA. Yeah, but it got real quiet in here all a sudden.

DOC. Patsy, get up there.

PATSY. Oh, I don't think I have an outfit for this.

DOC. Just wear anything.

PATSY. I'm on it.

(**PATSY** *exits into the dressing room.*)

ELDRIDGE. Look, it's like this: I'm a man of few words.

LUCINDA. And they're all pretty short, so this oughta be quick.

ELDRIDGE. What I'm trying to say...

(**ELDRIDGE** *turns to* **DOC.**)

DOC. Don't look at me.

(**ELDRIDGE** *turns to* **LUCINDA.** *He finally knows what to say.*)

ELDRIDGE. You remember how we met at the high school dance?

LUCINDA. Yes, I do. I remember it. There's pictures. We look real cute.

ELDRIDGE. And I saw you standin' in the corner, looking lonely. And I asked you why you weren't dancing. And you said you were waitin' for somebody to ask you.

LUCINDA. I said I didn't want to and go away.

ELDRIDGE. And I said maybe I'm that somebody.

LUCINDA. And I said maybe you oughta clean out your ears.

ELDRIDGE. But it was the last dance. And it started to rain. And you could either shut me up and dance, or go stand in the storm till Tommy come get you.

LUCINDA. And I gotta admit, you dance a heckuva lot better than a wet ball gown feels.

ELDRIDGE. They closed down the gym at half past ten, but we snuck across the street here to my daddy's bar and made whiskey sours till dawn. And free trips through the car wash.

LUCINDA. You kept trying to check my tire pressure.

ELDRIDGE. Thirty-five PSI. You thought I wouldn't remember.

(**LUCINDA** *giggles.*)

ELDRIDGE. All I ever wanted was for that thunderstorm to last forever.

LUCINDA. And here I'm just waitin' for a ray of sunshine.

ELDRIDGE. Maybe I'm that somebody.

LUCINDA. Life ain't the prom, El.

ELDRIDGE. All right, what about homecoming?

LUCINDA. Eldridge, give me one good reason why I would ever get back with you in a million years if hell froze over and you were the last man on earth. And I had amnesia.

(*MUSIC IN:* ***WHEN WE DANCE***)

(**PATSY** *enters in an old prom dress.*)

ELDRIDGE. Maybe this'll jog your memory.

(**ELDRIDGE** *pulls* **LUCINDA** *close, and they dance, just like they did back in high school. They are beautiful together. We finally understand what they maybe saw in each other once.*)

PATSY.

IT WAS HERE ON THIS OLD WOODEN DANCE FLOOR
THAT I FELL IN LOVE WITH YOU
WE'VE BEEN TOGETHER SINCE THAT NIGHT,
WE'VE LAUGHED AND CRIED LIKE LOVERS DO
AND WHENEVER WE NEED TO REMEMBER
THE FEELINGS WE FELT LONG BEFORE
WE HEAD DOWN TO THIS LITTLE DANCE HALL
AND SPEND THE NIGHT TAKING TURNS 'ROUND THE FLOOR

WHEN WE DANCE IT FEELS LIKE THE FIRST TIME
WHEN WE DANCE ALL THE YEARS SEEM TO FADE AWAY
WHEN WE NEED TO FALL IN LOVE AGAIN.
RECALL THE WAY IT WAS AGAIN
SAY ALL THE I LOVE YOUS THAT WE FORGET TO SAY
WE GET THE CHANCE WHEN WE DANCE

WHEN THEY'RE PUTTING THE CHAIRS ON THE TABLES
AND THE MUSIC JUST DISAPPEARS
YOU KNOW THAT WE'LL STILL BE SWAYING
TO A LOVE SONG NOBODY ELSE CAN HEAR

WHEN WE DANCE IT FEELS LIKE THE FIRST TIME
WHEN WE DANCE ALL THE YEARS SEEM TO FADE AWAY
WHEN WE NEED TO FALL IN LOVE AGAIN.
RECALL THE WAY IT WAS AGAIN
SAY ALL THE I LOVE YOUS THAT WE FORGET TO SAY
WE GET THE CHANCE WHEN WE DANCE

WHEN WE NEED TO FALL IN LOVE AGAIN
RECALL THE WAY IT WAS AGAIN
SAY ALL THE I LOVE YOUS THAT WE FORGET TO SAY
WE GET THE CHANCE WHEN WE DANCE

(**ELDRIDGE** *kisses* **LUCINDA.**)

ELDRIDGE. I always knew you'd come back to me.

LUCINDA. This ain't me coming back.

ELDRIDGE. She sure looks like you.

(**LUCINDA** *quietly pulls away.*)

LUCINDA. Eldridge, you maybe dance like you mean it. But that ain't how it works.

ELDRIDGE. Then why don't you remind me how it works?

(**ELDRIDGE** *tries to kiss her again, but* **DOC** *hauls off and punches him.*)

RODDY. Git him!

ELDRIDGE. What was that for?

LUCINDA. What's got into you, Doc?

DOC. I'm sorry, El. It's not your fault. I guess I'm just mad at myself.

ELDRIDGE. Well, your aim is lousy.

DOC. I'm sorry, Lucinda.

ELDRIDGE. What're you apologizing to her for?

LUCINDA. Can we talk about this later?

DOC. There's not gonna be a later. Cuz I'm leaving.

ELDRIDGE. Oh, no, you don't. Not till I get my crack at you.

(**ELDRIDGE** *takes a swing at* **DOC** *and misses.*)

ELDRIDGE. That was just a warning shot.

DOC. El, I'm your bartender. I handle unruly drunks for a living.

ELDRIDGE. Who you callin' unruly?

(**ELDRIDGE** *swings again and misses.*)

ELDRIDGE. Stop moving around!

LUCINDA. What do you mean, you're leaving, Doc?

DOC. I mean I'm leaving. For good.

LUCINDA. Just like that?

ELDRIDGE. You can't leave, you're working.

DOC. I'm not working, I quit.

ELDRIDGE. You can't quit, you're fired.

DOC. If I'm fired, I'm leaving.

LUCINDA. You're not leavin', it's raining. Just sit there and don't do anything crazy till I get back. Come on, El, let's get you bandaged up. Patsy, keep him outta the bar knives.

(*LUCINDA exits with* **ELDRIDGE** *to backstage.*)

PATSY. What the heck was that all about?

RODDY. I don't know. But it's been a long time coming.

PATSY. Doc, are you gonna be all right?

DOC. I been here my whole life, and it took me till just now to realize I don't belong.

PATSY. Course you do, Doc. You're as much a part of this place as El or Roddy or anyone. If it wasn't you, back behind the bar, like always, who'd keep Eldridge and Lucinda from tearing each other apart?

DOC. That's the problem. I've always been the third wheel that keeps them from being a real bicycle.

PATSY. I'm just going to put these bar knives in the cash register.

DOC. I got regulars come in every night wonderin' how the hell they wound up here. And I was too busy pourin' 'em answers to ask myself the same thing.

PATSY. Then why'd you stick around?

DOC. I guess I was hoping. Maybe deep down I did wonder what would've happened if Eldridge hadn't got to her first that night. Not that it would've mattered. I can't even walk straight. I couldn't dance to save my life.

PATSY. I thought you said you weren't there.

DOC. He kissed her in the rain, after the last dance, in the moonlight, and the rest is history. And a whole lot o' whiskey sours.

PATSY. But, Doc, you weren't there. Were you?

DOC. You see the way they are together. Like thunder and lightning. (*beat*) And I'm just the rain.

PATSY. I know what you mean, Doc. I had me a beagle got struck by thunder one time. *(sobs)* He never was right after that. Kept walkin' into doors. But I sure miss that dog.

DOC. You better get on stage, Patsy. The band's gettin' antsy. Now's your night. Better don't let her wait.

PATSY. Are you gonna be all right?

DOC. All right's a mite overrated, don'tcha think? Where'd you put those bar knives?

PATSY. I gotta go.

(**PATSY** *hurries back to the stage.*)

PATSY. *(to audience)* How y'all doing? Got a little rowdy in here, didn't it? I think y'all need to simmer back down again.

*(MUSIC IN: **I USED TO LOVE THE RAIN**)*

(**PATSY** *starts her song from the stage.* **DOC** *and* **LUCINDA** *join in from different parts of the bar.*)

PATSY.

THERE'S CLOUDS ROLLING IN, LOOKS LIKE RAIN
THE WIND'S BLOWING UP OUTSIDE
SEEMS TO ME LIKE IT'S GONNA BE
ANOTHER LONG COLD NIGHT

THERE'S A FLASH OF LIGHTNING
LIGHTING UP THE DISTANT SKY
AND WHEN THE THUNDER COMES,
IT MAKES ME WANT TO CRY

I USED TO LOVE THE RAIN
BEATING GENTLY ON THE WINDOW PANE
SAFE INSIDE WE'D HOLD EACH OTHER TIGHT
WITHOUT YOUR LOVE IT'S NOT THE SAME
USED TO LOVE THE RAIN

PATSY & DOC.

IT'S ONLY A STORM, IT'LL PASS ON BY
BEFORE THE MORNING LIGHT

PATSY & LUCINDA.

    IF I COULD SLEEP, I COULD KEEP

    THE TEARS OUT OF MY EYES

PATSY.

    USED TO SOUND LIKE MUSIC

    BUT NOW THE SONG HAS CHANGED

PATSY, DOC & LUCINDA.

    'CAUSE I'M ALONE AND

    IT JUST SOUNDS LIKE RAIN

PATSY.

    I USED TO LOVE THE RAIN

    BEATING GENTLY ON THE WINDOW PANE

    SAFE INSIDE WE'D HOLD EACH OTHER TIGHT

    WITHOUT YOUR LOVE IT'S NOT THE SAME

    USED TO LOVE THE RAIN

    WITHOUT YOUR LOVE IT'S NOT THE SAME

PATSY, DOC & LUCINDA.

    USED TO LOVE THE RAIN

PATSY. That didn't cheer me up at all.

*(**PATSY** runs off into the bathroom. **DOC** sulks behind the bar. No one's left on stage, really.)*

RODDY. Doc?

DOC. What?

RODDY. You want I should vamp?

DOC. Nobody cares what you do, Roddy.

RODDY. *(hurt)* My momma cares.

*(**DOC** turns away, leaving **RODDY** alone on stage. He's not comfortable there. But he does his best...)*

RODDY. Well, I guess that's our show, folks! *(He looks around, helplessly.)* We don't normally plan for it to end like this... But I guess that was wishful thinking. *(He hopes somebody will come back. They don't. He forges ahead.)* But if you come on back next week, who knows, maybe we'll have all the kinks ironed out by then. *(but somehow he doubts it)* Maybe they'll even let me do one o' my songs. *(**RODDY** realizes there's no one to stop him)* Unless you want to hear one right now?

(**RODDY** *pauses eagerly. Whatever the audience says…*)

RODDY. Customer's always right!

*(MUSIC IN: **WHATEVER'S LEFT OF ME**)*

(**RODDY** *sings his heart out. And back in again.*)

RODDY.

BABY, TIMES ARE HARD, EVERYBODY KNOWS IT
IT'S ALL THAT I CAN DO TO MAKE THE RENT
I WORK SIXTEEN HOURS A DAY,
'CAUSE I'VE GOT LOTS OF BILLS TO PAY
AND I ALWAYS WIND UP WONDERING JUST WHERE THE
    MONEY WENT

NOW, I THINK I'VE FOUND AN ANSWER TO OUR PROBLEM
CAN'T THINK OF ANY OTHER AND I'VE TRIED
THE GENTLEMAN I SAW SAYS IT AIN'T AGAINST THE LAW
AND HE'LL PAY ME WELL
SO HE CAN SELL
WHAT I'VE GOT INSIDE

SO I HOPE YOU'LL STILL BE WITH ME
WHEN I'VE ONLY GOT ONE KIDNEY
AND ONE LUNG AND ONE EYEBALL AND ONE KNEE
I MADE THE DEAL AND IN THE MORNIN'
I'LL BE LIGHT SOME VITAL ORGANS
AND DARLING I JUST HOPE THAT YOU'LL STILL LOVE
WHATEVER'S LEFT OF ME

AND WE'LL DO JUST FINE INVESTIN'
WHAT I GET FOR MY INTESTINE
HE SAYS HE'LL DO THE COLOSTOMY FOR FREE
WHAT THE HELL, IT DON'T WORK WELL AS FORMERLY
BUT MY PROSTATE'S STAYING WHERE IT'S SUPPOSED TO BE

SO I HOPE YOU'LL LOVE
WHATEVER'S LEFT OF ME

(**LUCINDA** *enters.*)

LUCINDA. Roddy, what the heck?

RODDY. *(sheepishly)* Sorry.

LUCINDA. What've you been told? Doc, why didn't you stop
him?

RODDY. Won't happen again.

PATSY. You gonna let her talk to you like that?

RODDY. That's how she talks.

PATSY. *(to* **LUCINDA***)* You know, Roddy's got feelin's, too, y'know.

LUCINDA. Eldridge is asking for you, Patsy.

PATSY. He is?

LUCINDA. No, but he's askin' for trouble if he tries to grope me one more time.

PATSY. I'm on it!

(**PATSY** *exits.*)

LUCINDA. *(to* **DOC***)* You're not for serious about leaving town all of a sudden?

DOC. I'd be a joke if I stayed.

LUCINDA. Where you gonna go?

DOC. How 'bout anyplace but here?

LUCINDA. Sounds exotic.

DOC. I'm sorry, Lucinda.

LUCINDA. Well, I'm sorry, too, Doc, but I hope you don't mind me dancing with the father of my child now and again. It's pretty much all we got.

DOC. You two deserve each other.

LUCINDA. Now that's uncalled for.

DOC. No, I mean it. You're good together.

LUCINDA. Sure. We go together like sparklers and kerosene. Makes for a heckuva 4th of July, but "Keep outta reach of children." *(beat)* Eldridge and me ain't never been much of a couple. You knew that from the wedding. But we got a history now. There's no denying that.

DOC. Nope.

LUCINDA. But you and me, Doc, we got a history, too.

DOC. This whole town's got history. Just not a lotta future.

LUCINDA. So you're just gonna go off and leave me here in it?

DOC. I can't ask you to come with me.

LUCINDA. Askin's always been your problem, Doc. Always trying so hard not to hurt a gal's feelings. When feelin's all she wants. *(beat)* Y'know, there's a reason you and me never got together in high school. And it's not cuz you wasn't there.

DOC. No, I know.

LUCINDA. And a gal in a prom dress can only wait so long.

(silence)

DOC. I was afraid you wouldn't want me, if I didn't have two good legs. But what I really shoulda had was the guts.

LUCINDA. Guts woulda been a good start.

*(**DOC** struggles to his feet.)*

DOC. Lucinda, you know I can't dance to save my life.

LUCINDA. No, I know.

*(**DOC** limps over to the dance floor. He turns to her.)*

DOC. But for you, I'd sure like to die trying.

LUCINDA. Now that's what I like to hear.

*(MUSIC IN: **LEAVE THE DANCIN' TO ME**)*

(She takes him by the hand and pulls him out to the middle of the dance floor.)

DOC. Be gentle?

LUCINDA. Not on your life.

(She spins him and catches him before he falls.)

LUCINDA.

BABY, YOU CAN'T DANCE, I KNOW IT'S TRUE
BUT THAT DON'T MATTER, I'M IN LOVE WITH YOU
SO COME OUT ON THE FLOOR AND WHEN YOU DO
JUST LEAVE THE DANCING TO ME

YOU GOT TWO LEFT FEET, HONEY I DON'T CARE
I NEVER PLANNED TO MEET NO FRED ASTAIRE
SO DON'T BE SHY, AND DON'T GET SCARED,
JUST LEAVE THE DANCING TO ME

LEAVE THE DANCING TO ME

YOU'RE THE KIND OF GUY
WHO CAN'T SHAKE HIS HIPS
BUT I LOVE YOUR EYES
AND I LOVE YOUR LIPS
AND IN YOUR ARMS IS WHERE I WANT TO BE
YOU GOT NO MOVES, YOU CAN'T DO NO FLIPS
BUT EVEN IF YOU ONLY WIGGLE YOUR FINGER TIPS
GET OFF YOUR CHAIR, I WANT YOU THERE WITH ME

BABY, YOU CAN'T DANCE, YOU DON'T GLIDE AROUND
BUT THERE'S NOTHING LIKE THE LOVE WE FOUND
SO COME OUT ON THE FLOOR,
STAND YOUR GROUND
AND JUST LEAVE THE DANCING TO ME

(Throughout the song, **LUCINDA** *dances circles around* **DOC**. *She dances for him. She dances with him. And in the end, she maybe even gets him to shake a leg himself.)*

YOU'RE THE KIND OF GUY
WHO CAN'T SHAKE HIS HIPS
BUT I LOVE YOUR EYES
AND I LOVE YOUR LIPS
AND IN YOUR ARMS IS WHERE I WANT TO BE
YOU GOT NO MOVES, YOU CAN'T DO NO FLIPS
BUT EVEN IF YOU ONLY WIGGLE YOUR FINGER TIPS
GET OFF YOUR CHAIR, I WANT YOU THERE WITH ME

BABY, YOU CAN'T DANCE, BUT THAT'S OKAY
YOU KNOW I'D NEVER TRADE YOU ANYWAY
SO HOLD ME TIGHT WHILE THE MUSIC PLAYS
AND JUST LEAVE THE DANCING TO ME

LEAVE THE DANCING TO ME
LEAVE THE DANCING TO ME

*(***DOC*** kisses ***LUCINDA***.)*

DOC. Y'know, I could get used to liking this.

LUCINDA. See, that wasn't so bad.

DOC. We shoulda done this years ago.

LUCINDA. Yeah. That's probably when we shoulda done it.

(**LUCINDA** *quietly pulls away.*)

DOC. What's the matter?

LUCINDA. I'm sorry, Doc, I oughta go, it's gettin' late. And I got work in the mornin'...

DOC. You got work on Monday.

LUCINDA. And I got Roddy comin' by for that clutch...

DOC. You're not runnin' out on runnin' off with me, are you?

LUCINDA. Well, what do you want us to do? Just hop on the highway and don't look back?

DOC. Now who's afraid of hoppin'?

LUCINDA. I'm sorry, Doc, but you're right, I can't just up and leave. I got family here. And El-three to think about...

DOC. I'm not sayin' you gotta drop everything and run off with me right this second. But would you ever?

LUCINDA. Ever's a long time.

DOC. Never's a lot longer.

LUCINDA. And if I say "someday?" What do we do till then?

DOC. I don't know.

LUCINDA. I don't know, either.

DOC. But maybe that's the best thing for us.

LUCINDA. Not knowing?

DOC. Every night of my whole life I knew exactly where I was gonna be the next morning. And it's always got me nowhere. But now it's all up in the air. And it's the closest I ever been to flying.

LUCINDA. We're still trapped here in this miserable God-forsaken town.

DOC. Nah, it only looks that way when you're standin' in the middle of it. Watchin' cars go by on the interstate. But starting tonight, you and me, we're just passin' through. We're just passin' time.

LUCINDA. And we're itchin' to leave.

DOC. And that's gonna make all the difference. Cuz one o' these nights, the time'll be right, and I'm parked right outside.

(**DOC** *puts his car keys in a glass on the bar.*)

(*MUSIC IN:* ***TOURISTS***)

DOC. And then we'll be the ones watchin' our troubles go by in the rear view mirror. Puttin' the past behind us like it was just standin' still.

(*sings*)

NOW BABY, LOOK AT THEM ON THE AVENUE
THEY'RE ALL ON FIRE TONIGHT
CHASING LOVE THE WHOLE NIGHT THROUGH
HOPING SOMETHING TURNS OUT RIGHT

AND IN EACH PAIR OF EYES YOU SEE
THE SAME UNSPOKEN NEED
LIKE A PRISONER WAITING FOR
THE DAY HE WILL BE FREED

SO TAKE A LONG LOOK BABY,
THEN LET'S WALK AWAY FOR GOOD
THERE'S NOTHING FOR US ANYMORE
IN THIS OLD NEIGHBORHOOD

NOW WE HAVE EACH OTHER
TAKE MY HAND AND HOLD IT TIGHT
I'M SINCERELY GLAD THAT WE'RE
JUST TOURISTS HERE TONIGHT

LUCINDA.

THE GIRLS ARE STILL ALL DRESSED TO KILL
THE GUYS LAUGH A LITTLE TOO LOUD
EVERYBODY'S WONDERING IF THEY WILL

LUCINDA & DOC.

FIND SOMEONE IN THE CROWD

LUCINDA.

MAYBE WE CAN DO IT
SEEMS LIKE JUST YESTERDAY
I WAS AFRAID THAT I WOULD NEVER
HEAR SOMEBODY SAY.....

LUCINDA & DOC.
> JUST TAKE A LONG LOOK BABY
> THEN LET'S WALK AWAY

LUCINDA.
> FOR GOOD

LUCINDA & DOC.
> THERE'S NOTHING FOR US HERE

LUCINDA.
> IN THIS HARD-HEARTED NEIGHBORHOOD
> OUR LOVE CAN SHINE MORE BRIGHTLY
> THAN A THOUSAND FLASHING LIGHTS

LUCINDA & DOC.
> I'M SINCERELY GLAD THAT WE'RE
> JUST TOURISTS HERE TONIGHT

LUCINDA.
> I'M SINCERELY GLAD THAT WE'RE
> JUST TOURISTS HERE TONIGHT

> *(Music continues under, as they kiss.)*

DOC. So you wanna say "someday?"

LUCINDA. I'm sorry, Doc. But I've had enough o' "someday" to last a lifetime.

> *(**LUCINDA** scoops up the car keys and heads for the door.)*

LUCINDA. But I could sure use some "right about now."

> *(**LUCINDA** tosses the keys to **DOC.**)*

DOC. What about Eldridge?

LUCINDA. What about him?

DOC. I couldn'ta said it better.

> *(He takes her in his arms and kisses her. **ELDRIDGE** enters with both eyes bandaged. **PATSY** helps him to the stage. She spies **DOC** and **LUCINDA** as they head for the door.)*

PATSY. Uh oh.

ELDRIDGE. What oh?

PATSY. Eldridge, you better not look.

ELDRIDGE. I can't look, Patsy.

PATSY. That's probably best.

ELDRIDGE. Why? What's going on?

(**DOC** and **LUCINDA** *wave to* **RODDY** *and* **PATSY** *as they exit through the kitchen.*)

PATSY. It's nothing. Lucinda's dancin' with somebody, that's all.

ELDRIDGE. Patsy, that girl is always gonna be dancin' with somebody.

PATSY. Well, what if it ain't just anybody?

ELDRIDGE. If it ain't anybody, who does that leave? Roddy!?

RODDY. What?

ELDRIDGE. What'd I tell you 'bout makin' time with my Lucinda?

RODDY. Then how come Doc gets to do it?

ELDRIDGE. Because he– What?!

PATSY. Roddy!

RODDY. What?

PATSY. Don't tell him that!

RODDY. He shouldn'ta asked.

(**ELDRIDGE** *tears at his bandages.*)

PATSY. Now, Eldridge, you gotta calm down. You don't wanna sprain your eyes.

ELDRIDGE. Let go of me, Patsy! My best man's makin' off with my best girl. I been waitin' ten years for this.

PATSY. You been what?

(**ELDRIDGE** *rips off his bandages and runs to the door.*)

ELDRIDGE. (*shouts out the door*) That's right, you better run! And keep on runnin'!

(**DOC** *enters, walks past* **ELDRIDGE**, *fetches Lucinda's purse.*)

DOC. Forgot her purse.

(**DOC** *exits.*)

ELDRIDGE. *(shouts out the door)* And don't even think about come crawlin' back here!

*(**LUCINDA** enters, walks past **ELDRIDGE**, fetches her drink from the bar.)*

LUCINDA. Night, El.

*(She exits. **ELDRIDGE** sulks.)*

RODDY. I thought those two would never figure themselves out.

*(**PATSY** gingerly approaches **ELDRIDGE**.)*

PATSY. Eldridge, are you gonna be all right?

*(**ELDRIDGE** thinks about it.)*

ELDRIDGE. Aw, hell, I owe him a Jeep. I'm just glad it's not some city boy off a tour bus. *(to audience)* You know who you are.

PATSY. So you're not gonna be all mad and all?

ELDRIDGE. Patsy, don't you know there's more important things in life?? We got a show to do!

*(**ELDRIDGE** puts the bandages back on his eyes.)*

ELDRIDGE. Now point me which way to the stage. I got a crowd to please.

*(**PATSY** turns him in the right direction.)*

PATSY. Are you sure you're ready for this?

ELDRIDGE. Patsy, how many times I gotta tell you? Ready's where I was born. *(to audience)* Ladies and Gentlemen… funny thing happened on the way to the honky tonk. Not so funny for me, cuz I'm the one got jumped by a coupla big fellas comin' out a dark alley.

PATSY. You what?

ELDRIDGE. But if you think this looks bad, you oughta see the other guys. *(points at one eye)* This one walks with a limp now. *(points at his other eye, shrugs)* And the other one's gay. Ha ha! Roddy, don't you dare hold me back.

*(MUSIC IN: **WE GOTTA LOTTA ROCKIN' TO DO**)*

(**ELDRIDGE** *leaps back up on stage like he never left.*)

ELDRIDGE.

WELL EVERY TIME I HEAR SOMEBODY
TELL ME THAT I GOTTA TAKE IT EASY,
GOTTA TAKE IT SLOW
YOU KNOW IT MAKES ME WONDER
WHY THEY WANT TO PULL ME UNDER
BEFORE I'M REALLY READY TO GO
WELL THEY CAN SIT RIGHT BACK IN THEIR EASY CHAIR
AND GO TO SLEEP BY THE TV LIGHT
BUT, BABY THEY AIN'T NEVER GONNA FIND US THERE
'CAUSE WE GOT BETTER THINGS TO DO TONIGHT

WELL ME AND YOU WE GOTTA LOTTA ROCKIN' TO DO
IT AIN'T OVER 'TIL IT'S OVER,
WE AIN'T THROUGH 'TIL WE'RE THROUGH
PUT ON THAT TIGHT RED DRESS
AND THOSE DANCIN' SHOES
'CAUSE ME AND YOU WE GOTTA LOTTA ROCKIN' TO DO

HEY, WE MAY NOT BE AS YOUNG AS WE BOTH USED TO BE
BUT BABY I'M NOT EVEN COUNTING, NEITHER ARE YOU
AND THE WAY YOU LOOK WHENEVER YOU COME OUT WITH
    ME;
WELL, YOU COULD SHOW 'EM ALL A THING OR TWO
SO LET 'EM TUNE IN THEIR OLD RADIO
TO WHERE THE MUSIC'S NICE AND LIGHT
WE GOT NO USE FOR SOMETHING SOFT AND SLOW
'CAUSE YOU KNOW WE'RE GONNA PARTY TONIGHT

ME AND YOU WE GOTTA LOTTA ROCKIN' TO DO
IT AIN'T OVER 'TIL IT'S OVER,
WE AIN'T THROUGH 'TIL WE'RE THROUGH
PUT ON THAT TIGHT RED DRESS
AND THOSE DANCIN' SHOES
'CAUSE ME AND YOU WE GOTTA LOTTA ROCKIN' TO DO

ELDRIDGE. *(cont.)*

A LOTTA ROCKIN', A LOTTA ROCKIN' TO DO
PUT ON THAT TIGHT RED DRESS
AND THOSE DANCIN' SHOES
'CAUSE ME AND YOU WE GOTTA LOTTA ROCKIN' TO DO

A LOTTA ROCKIN', A LOTTA ROCKIN' TO DO
PUT ON THAT TIGHT RED DRESS
AND THOSE DANCIN' SHOES
'CAUSE ME AND YOU WE GOTTA LOTTA ROCKIN' TO DO

ME AND YOU WE GOTTA LOTTA ROCKIN' TO DO

*(The crowd goes wild.)**

END OF PLAY

---

* See Apendix 2 and 3 for additional optional songs.

APPENDIX 1

The part of Lucinda was originally conceived as a role for a virtuoso dancer, while Patsy was the show's primary songbird. This specialization was established in part to make sure the play would be easy to cast in communities where triple-threat singer/dancer/actors might be a rarity.

Premiering the musical in Los Angeles, however, the availability of professional singer/dancers was not really an issue, so we expanded the roles of both Patsy – choreographing her into several of the dance numbers – and Lucinda to show off the talents of our actors.

For the 2010 remount, songwriter Richard Levinson created an additional solo for Lucinda to feature the vocal talents of the female lead.

Optional Song - "Too Early for the Blues" - page 28

DOC. Grew up. Stopped dreaming. Same difference.

> (**DOC** *pours* **LUCINDA** *another drink.*)

> (*MUSIC IN:* ***TOO EARLY FOR THE BLUES***)

LUCINDA.
> YOU'RE NOT SUPPOSED TO GET THE BLUES THIS EARLY
> YOU'RE NOT SUPPOSED TO FEEL SAD SO SOON
> THAT CLOCK UP ON THE BAR BACK WALL
> SAYS I HAVEN'T DANCED NEAR 'NUFF AT ALL
> OR HAD A CHANCE TO CALL MY FAVORITE TUNE

> YOU'RE NOT SUPPOSED TO FEEL ALONE 'TIL LATER
> BUT TONIGHT MY HEART JUST DIDN'T GET THE NEWS
> THEY SAY THAT GOOD TIMES NEVER LAST
> BUT NOT SUFFICIENT TIME HAS PAST
> RIGHT NOW IT'S MUCH TOO EARLY FOR THE BLUES

> I KNOW THAT THEY ARE GONNA TAKE ME DOWN TONIGHT
> BUT THAT AIN'T ON MY SCHEDULE JUST YET
> AND I DON'T PLAN ON GIVIN' UP WITHOUT A FIGHT
> THESE NEW LUCCHESE BOOTS I GOT WILL KNOCK THEM
>   FLAT I BET

> SOMETIMES I THINK I COME IN HERE JUST TO GET MY HURT
>   ON
> AND FIND OUT JUST HOW LONG A GIRL CAN TAKE IT
> SOMETIMES I THINK THAT I AM ONE BIG NERVE WITH A
>   SKIRT ON

BUT IF I DON'T FEEL SO GOOD FOR REAL,
IT FEELS REAL GOOD TO FAKE IT

NO, YOU'RE NOT SUPPOSED TO CRY 'TIL NIGHT IS OVER
AND AS LONG AS I CAN STAND UP, I CAN CHOOSE
SO LET 'EM HIT ME WITH THE BEST THEY GOT
I'LL BE FINE UNTIL I'M NOT
RIGHT NOW IT'S MUCH TOO EARLY FOR THE BLUES
YES, NOW IT'S MUCH TOO EARLY FOR THE BLUES

(Like a dog baying after music, **RODDY** *suddenly bursts into song:)*

*(MUSIC IN: **WHATEVER'S LEFT OF ME**)*

RODDY.
BABY, TIMES ARE HARD, EVERYBODY KNOWS IT...

APPENDIX 2

For the critically-acclaimed 2009 production of *Savin' Up for Saturday Night* at Sacred Fools Theater in Los Angeles, director Jeremy Aldridge conceived an environmental staging of the play, converting the 99-seat theatre into an actual working bar serving up drinks throughout the show.

One of the necessities of the environmental staging was a server to deliver the aforementioned drinks and it quickly became apparent that the actor playing Patsy, the waitress in the play, would be unable to serve in that practical capacity since she would be too busy doing the play to take drink orders.

So an additional chorus member was cast as a hostess to greet the audience as they came in the door, make sure they found their seats, chat 'em up, and bring 'em a beer and a quart of motor oil.

We nicknamed the character Sissy and she essentially became the emcee of the show's framing device, so songwriter Richard Levinson wrote an additional solo for her to perform at the end of the evening as a coda to the play and a button to her own performance. Sissy sang *Here* while she closed up the bar after Eldridge and the others had left the stage at the end of the play.

Optionally, *Here* could be sung by Patsy or Roddy in a production that did not include a chorus or a hostess/narrator.

Coda - Here

HERE - *music & lyrics by Richard Levinson*

THE FIRST TIME THAT I CAME THROUGH THAT DOOR
EVERYTHING BECAME QUITE CLEAR
LIKE NOWHERE THAT I'D EVER BEEN BEFORE
I KNEW I'D LOVE IT HERE

THE FIRST TIME SOMEONE SMILED AND SAID HELLO
WELL THAT JUST BLEW AWAY ALL MY FEAR
AND SOON I WANTED EVERYONE TO KNOW
THAT I JUST LOVED IT HERE

DON'T WANT TO MAKE TOO BIG A DEAL ABOUT IT
PEOPLE HERE ARE JUST LIKE ANYONE
SOMETIMES THEY DISAPPOINT ME
SOMETIMES THEY MAKE ME MAD
SOMETIMES I THINK IT'S TIME TO CUT AND RUN
BUT THEN I LOOK AROUND AT THIS LIFE I SOMEHOW
    FOUND

AND IN EACH FAMILIAR FACE I SEE
JUST WHAT THIS PLACE NOW MEANS TO ME

AND I KNOW SOMEDAY
WE'RE ALL JUST GONNA DISAPPEAR
SO I WANT TO TAKE THE TIME RIGHT NOW TO SAY
I REALLY LOVE IT HERE
I REALLY LOVE IT HERE

APPENDIX 3

For the original production at Sacred Fools Theater in Los Angeles, after the curtain call, we added a reprise of the title song and cast members encouraged the audience to get up and dance along with them, which made for a rousing finale to an interactive evening.

*(Encore - **SAVIN' UP FOR SATURDAY NIGHT (REPRISE)**)*

*(After the curtain call, **ELDRIDGE** returns to the stage.)*

ELDRIDGE. Well, you all been such a great crowd, so we're gonna see if we can't get the band to do us one more. But it looks like there's still a couple o' you thinkin' about sittin' the last one out. So let me remind you: It's like the good doctor says: It don't matter one bit if you don't got the moves. Just as long as you get up the guts. Roddy?

*(MUSIC IN: **SAVIN' UP FOR SATURDAY NIGHT (REPRISE)**)*

(The whole cast comes back for one more. They dance with the audience.)

ELDRIDGE (& COMPANY).
    I'M SAVING UP FOR SATURDAY NIGHT
    THAT'S THE BEST THAT I CAN DO
    ECONOMICALLY SPEAKIN'
    I'M JUST WORKING FOR THE WEEKEND
    WHEN I HIT THE TOWN WITH YOU
    WHEN FRIDAY'S HERE IT'S VERY CLEAR
    MY FUTURE'S LOOKIN' BRIGHT
    'CAUSE I'M A MAN WITH A FINANCIAL PLAN
    I'M SAVING UP FOR SATURDAY NIGHT

    NOW I DON'T PLAY THE MARKET
    LIKE OTHER GUYS I KNOW
    MY TAB DOWN AT THE HONKY-TONK
    THAT'S MY PORTFOLIO
    I DON'T HAVE AN ACCOUNTANT
    BUT, BABY THAT'S ALRIGHT
    HE'D JUST SAY NOW CALL YOUR GIRL

YOU CAN TAKE HER FOR A WHIRL
'CAUSE YOU GOT JUST ENOUGH FOR SATURDAY NIGHT

I'M SAVING UP FOR SATURDAY NIGHT
THAT'S THE BEST THAT I CAN DO
ECONOMICALLY SPEAKIN'
I'M JUST WORKING FOR THE WEEKEND
WHEN I HIT THE TOWN WITH YOU
WHEN FRIDAY'S HERE IT'S VERY CLEAR
MY FUTURE'S LOOKIN' BRIGHT
I'M A MAN WITH A FINANCIAL PLAN
I'M SAVING UP FOR SATURDAY NIGHT

AND IF I BLOW IT ALL,
AT LEAST WE'LL HAVE A BALL,
SAVING UP FOR SATURDAY NIGHT

YEAH, IF I BLOW IT ALL,
AT LEAST WE'LL HAVE A BALL,
SAVING UP FOR SATURDAY NIGHT

LAST CALL!